Two for Vengeance

OTHER SAGEBRUSH LARGE PRINT WESTERNS BY
LEWIS B. PATTEN

Ambush Creek
Feud at Chimmey Rock
No God in Saguaro

Two for Vengeance

LEWIS B. PATTEN

Library of Congress Cataloging-in-Publication Data

Patten, Lewis B.
Two for vengeance / Lewis B. Patten
p. cm.
ISBN 1-57490-309-8 (lg. print : hardcover)
1. Large type books. I. Title

PS3556.A79 T88 2000
813'.54—dc21 00-059154

Cataloguing in Publication Data is available from
the British Library and the National Library of Australia.

Sagebrush Large Print Westerns are published in the United States and Canada by Thomas T. Beeler, Publisher, PO Box 659, Hampton Falls, New Hampshire 03844-0659. ISBN 1-57490-309-8

Published in the United Kingdom, Eire, and the Republic of South Africa by Isis Publishing Ltd, 7 Centremead, Osney Mead, Oxford OX2 0ES England. ISBN 0-7531-6369-1

Published in Australia and New Zealand by Bolinda Publishing Pty Ltd, 17 Mohr Street, Tullamarine, Victoria, Australia 3043
ISBN 1-74030-210-9

Manufactured by Sheridan Books in Chelsea, Michigan.

CHAPTER 1

AT SUNDOWN THEY CAME RIDING HOME, BIG JESS Hawkins and his son, from a day of greasing windmills out on the windswept plain. The first thing they saw was the empty corral, its gate ajar, the buggy horse gone. And they saw too the milch cow standing bawling beside the barn, waiting to be milked.

Unusual, but no real reason for the sudden great uneasiness that came to Jess, making him feel cold and empty and afraid.

Impulse made him jab spurs into his horse's sides. Reluctance to frighten Abe unnecessarily made him haul back on the reins at once. The confused horse crow-hopped as if he didn't know what to do.

Hawkins eased off on the reins, and the horse broke into a trot. Down the long slope they came, Hawkins' eyes now narrow and intense. He was looking for movement, but except for the white chickens scratching there in the yard, he could see none.

He saw color, though. A patch of blue—sky blue—and near it something white, and not far from that, two tiny spots of red. The twins had been wearing red today. His wife had been wearing blue.

His heart told him what those spots of color were, but his mind refused to acknowledge it. Things were civilized out here now. The Indians were peaceable, living on their reservations and bothering nobody anymore.

He wanted to tell Abe to wait, because be was somehow sure what they were going to find. Yet he knew the boy would argue, and he had no time for argument. He spurred his horse again, leaving a startled Abe behind. He thundered down the last quarter-mile and into the barren, dusty yard.

His first uneasy premonition had been right. Yet, still he could not accept the truth. He left his horse in a single leap, and the animal skidded to a halt, snorting and rolling his eyes because of the smell of death.

Jess Hawkins ran to the body of his wife, staked out naked on the ground, hands and feet spread, wrists and ankles bloody because of her struggling. He threw himself down beside her and laid his face against hers and found it cold.

He was stunned and shocked and silent for a long, long time. Then a great, agonized cry was wrenched out of him, a wordless, animal cry of pain. He had forgotten Abe. He had forgotten everything but the horror of what had happened here. Her body was dusty, soiled, ravaged; and seeing it that way was like having a knife buried in his gut.

How does the mind of man comprehend such a sudden and horrifying thing? It is slow and hard. But the mind does absorb it finally, even if it cannot wholly accept it yet. Jess rose as if in a daze, remembering the two tiny spots of red. He went to them and found that they were the bodies of the five-year-old twins, their red dresses soiled and dusty too.

He heard a retching sound, and looked, and saw Abe bent double, heaving out the contents of his stomach on the ground. Abe's face was greenish, his eyes like those of a stricken animal. Suddenly Jess Hawkins knew Abe needed him more than did these dead. He went to him and put his hand on his forehead and held it there until Abe had finished vomiting. Then he put his big, strong arms around his son and held him close, despite the fact that he was fifteen and almost as tall as Jess.

Abe's body shook as if he had a chill. His teeth chattered, yet from between his chattering teeth came sobs, torn from away down deep, and full of agony.

Jess Hawkins finally pushed his son away. He gripped Abe's shoulders with fingers that bit in and hurt. He said harshly, "Go to the barn! Milk that goddamn cow!"

Abe stared at him, surprised, but he said dutifully, "Yes, sir," and left, staggering like someone who has had too much to drink.

He went halfway to the barn and turned. "We got to get after them."

Jess said, "Milk the cow. We got to give our dead some respect."

"What should I do with the milk?"

Jess started to say, "Take it to the house," but then he stopped. He said, "Dump it on the ground."

Abe turned and headed for the barn again. Jess Hawkins fished out his pocketknife and cut the ropes that bound his wife's wrists and ankles to the stakes. He gently lifted her and carried her to the house. He took her to their bed and laid her down and covered her. He sat with her a little while, tears welling out of his eyes and running across his weathered cheeks.

He had to tear himself away. He went out when he was able, picked up the twins one by one, and gently carried each into the house. He laid them outside the covers, one on each side of his wife. Outside again, he picked up what remained of his wife's blue dress, and her other clothes, and carried them inside the house.

The three bodies lay side-by-side on the bed. Suddenly something in Jess Hawkins finally gave way. Sobs were torn from him, sobs beyond his ability to control. It was the first time he had really wept since he had been a little boy. He bent double, almost convulsed, and he was able only partially to control himself when he heard Abe's footsteps on the stairs. He wiped his face with his hands. He clenched his fists and fought for self-control.

Turning, he saw Abe standing in the bedroom door. The boy's face was white, his eyes confused. "Pa, what we going to do?"

"We'll dig their graves. We'll sit up the night with them, and tomorrow we'll bury them."

"What about whoever it was that done this to them?"

"In due time, son"

Abe stared at him, white-faced, defiant. "What about now, Pa? What about right now? Before they get away."

Jess Hawkins said, "They ain't going to get away."

Abe said, "Goddamnit, Pa!"

It was the first time Jess had heard profanity pass his lips. He said, "You'll mind your tongue!"

"Yes, sir." But the defiance remained in Abe's eyes, along with growing puzzlement.

Jess Hawkins said, "Sit here with them. I'll start yhe graves. When I come back, then you can dig."

Abe looked scared. He said, "Pa ..."

"Sit with them, son. They're not fearful, They're only your family."

Jess Hawkins went out and down the stairs. He got a shovel from the barn, went to a spot on the hillside where Edie had liked to sit when she had time, and began to dig. He dug with a single-minded ferocity, as if only violent physical work could dull the pain in him. He attacked the earth as if it was responsible for the deaths of his wife and two little girls.

He was down six feet deep on his wife's grave before

he even paused, panting raggedly, bathed with sweat. He was near collapse. He leaned on the side of the grave and rested, discovering that exhaustion *could* dull the pain, and had.

He laid the shovel crossways to the grave on top of the ground and swung out of it. He walked down to the house. Exhaustion might have dulled the pain; it had also done something else. It had made going on seem bleak and empty and meaningless. Edie was dead, his mind kept repeating. Edie was dead. Edie was dead.

And the little girls, so pretty, so innocent and sweet. They were also gone. No more would they put their tiny arms around his neck, no more lay their petal-soft faces against his own rough, grizzled one. They needn't have been killed. They couldn't have interfered. But they had screamed with terror, and they had been killed to silence them.

Abe was sitting where Jess had left him. His face was white, his eyes stricken. There were the streaks of tears upon his face. Jess said, "Go dig. Make the girls' graves no bigger than needed, one on each side of your mother's grave."

The boy got up. "Yes, sir." He was plainly relieved to get out of the house, relieved to have something to do. Jess watched him go, then pulled the chair close to the bed and sat down.

Death had relaxed his wife's face, which must have been contorted with pain and terror when she died. Jess stared at it. The years stretched ahead of him, empty and without purpose now that she was gone.

He remembered young Abe's words suddenly, "We got to get after them."

For now, that would be purpose enough for his life. Catching the men who had done this to his wife, who had murdered his little girls to shut them up.

Tonight he would sit with his wife and little girls. In the morning he and Abe would bury them. When that was done, they would pick up the trail and follow it, and no matter how long it took, they would catch each and every man who had helped commit this awful crime.

Jess Hawkins did not have to think long about turning the problem over to the law, because that would be the same as doing nothing. The law was an often drunk and always ineffectual sheriff in a tiny town fifteen miles away. The sheriff would send a few telegrams, and that was all that he would do.

Abe came back when the sky turned dark. He was sweaty and covered with earth, and he was plainly tired. "They're done, Pa."

Jess Hawkins nodded.

"Pa, hadn't we ought to eat?"

He almost scolded Abe, that he could think of food at a time like this. He stifled what he might have said. They hadn't eaten since morning. They both were tired. Eating would be no sacrilege, and they'd need their strength for what was ahead. He said, "Yes. You stay here, and I'll go fix something."

The kitchen had been rifled, everything edible taken away. Jess went out to the root cellar. He found potatoes, and lard, and a piece of antelope meat, and carried them into the house. He built up the fire in the stove, and when it was hot, sliced meat and potatoes and put them on to fry.

When everything was ready, he called to Abe. The boy came downstairs. He didn't say anything, but sat down to eat. When both were finished, Jess Hawkins said, "Clean up the table. I'll go sit with them."

He went up the stairs. He lighted no lamp, but sat in

the darkness. He was remembering Edie as she had been as a girl, and he was remembering what she had looked like the day he married her. He remembered driving here to stake their homestead claim in a wagon piled high with everything they owned.

He remembered the nights he had lain beside her, and he remembered her laughter and her tears. He had helped her bear the twins, himself being midwife because they bad come suddenly and unexpectedly.

Theirs had been a closeness of spirit that, though Jess did not know it, was rare in marriages. Thinking of her, he wept again there in the darkness, stifling the sobs only when he heard Abe coming up the stairs.

Abe said, "Pa?"

"Yes."

"What should I do?"

"Corral the horses and feed them. Get some food together for tomorrow. There's money under the loose hearthstone. Get that, and get the rifle and my pistol and your twenty-two and all the ammunition we have for them. Get blankets and extra clothes."

"Yes, sir." Abe went on back down the stairs.

Jess did not move, but sat there staring toward the bed where his wife and daughters lay. Not again would he come back to this place. Perhaps he would sell it if the money ran out before he had accomplished what he was about to undertake.

He could hear Abe moving around downstairs. His eyes were dry now. The agony was still there in his heart, but he had it under control. It was a cold core of fury now, fury that would show no mercy toward the ones who had done this thing.

The night passed slowly. Abe came up when he had done what he had been told to do, and Jess said, "Sleep,

Abe, if you can. There is a hard day ahead of us."

He didn't know whether his son slept or not. He didn't. He couldn't. He sat the night through, staring bleakly at nothing, and when dawn grayed the eastern sky, he dressed his wife in her best, lifted her, and carried her outside and up the hill to her final resting place. Returning, he brought the twins, one by one, and after that, blankets to wrap them in.

He jumped down into the graves and lifted them in, and climbed out and took the Bible out of young Abe's hands.

He read, "The Lord giveth and the Lord taketh away. Blessed be the name of the Lord."

Blessed? Where had the Lord been yesterday when this good woman and these two innocent children had met death at the hands of a savage gang of murderers? He thought of another passage in the good book. "Vengeance is mine, saith the Lord."

Well, the Lord had failed to protect Edie and the girls. He would not now avenge them. That was Jess Hawkins' job. And Abe's.

CHAPTER 2

JESS HAWKINS SENT ABE TO SADDLE THE HORSES before he began filling in the graves. He told him to put the provisions in gunnysacks and load them along with the guns, ammunition, and blankets. He told him to hang a sack of oats on each saddle and then to wait.

It took all the will he had to throw the first shovel of earth into his wife's grave. He knew Abe couldn't have stood it without breaking down.

When the bodies were completely covered, it was

easier. He filled the graves and mounded them over. Then he walked to the barn, sweating but not at all tired, because the stimulus of what he had to do was beginning to work on him. He made three small crosses out of wood, wrote the names and dates on them, then carried them back up the hill and pushed them down into the earth.

He stood for a moment. His wife and his two little girls were dead. No amount of grieving was going to bring them back. But their deaths cried out to be avenged.

Yet vengeance was not the only reason Jess Hawkins was going after the murderers. How many times, he asked himself, had this same thing happened before, to other women and children, in other places where this bunch of human wolves had stopped? And how many times would it happen again if they were not eliminated now?

He went down the hill and returned the shovel to its accustomed place in the barn. He walked out, then, clear of the yard, which was a mass of foot and hoof prints, until, circling, he found the tracks of the killers coming in, later found them leaving on the opposite side of the yard. They were heading southeast. He knelt and studied the prints, memorizing each set, memorizing each flaw and inequality of shoe or hoof. They were not Indians. He knew that instantly, because some of their horses were shod, though none recently. He counted. There were seven of them in all, plus the stolen buggy horse.

Seven, he thought with horror. Seven had raped and abused Edie, and then, when they were through with her, had killed her brutally so that she could never point the finger of guilt at them. Maybe that was why they had also killed the twins. So that the two could never point then out.

Abe had the horses ready by the time he reached the house. He checked everything. Abe had forgotten canteens, so he got two, filled them at the well, and hung one on each saddle. Abe had his twenty-two. Jess had his old navy percussion revolver and his rifle, a repeating Winchester.

Abe told him that the money was gone. That didn't surprise him. With the twins threatened, Edie wouldn't have hesitated about telling them where it was.

He took the lead, walking his horse. He picked up the trail and followed it easily. From behind, Abe called, "Hadn't we ought to hurry, Pa?"

He glanced around. He wanted to hurry too. His anger demanded it, but he knew haste might defeat them instead of help. He said, "It happened yesterday. That bunch didn't ride all through the night. I figure we ain't no more than six or seven hours behind."

"If we hurried, we could catch up to them."

"And what would we do then? There's seven of them, and we're only two."

"We could kill some of them before they got both of us."

Jess Hawkins said coldly, "I don't want some of them. I want them all."

Both his tone and his words made their impression on Abe, who since last night had been critical of the delay. Perhaps he was facing, in his own mind, the difficulties involved in two going up against seven such as these.

They plodded across the plain. Abe looked back before the house and buildings went out of sight, as if permanently fixing the sight in his mind. But Jess did not. He felt as though he never wanted to see it again.

Coldness was growing in him in spite of his anger

and the warmth of the sun. He fought a constant fight—to keep the sight of Edie, lying there staked to the ground, out of his thoughts. He fought a constant fight to keep from remembering how the twins had looked lying there.

Only coldness could drive out that kind of thoughts. Only thinking of what he meant to do to the men when he caught them could make him stop remembering.

Near noon, they found the place where the seven had camped last night. Jess stopped only long enough to study the boot tracks of the seven men. When he mounted to go on, be knew each individual boot track as well as he knew each horse's track.

All afternoon they rode, now at a trot to close the distance separating them from their prey. The killers' horses were walking. From the looks of the prints of their hooves and shoes, they had been traveling for a long, long time. Without substantial rest, without pause even long enough to fit them with new shoes.

Jess wondered what they were running from. A robbery, perhaps. Or a killing. Or maybe they were going *to* someplace instead of away from it.

They camped when the sky turned dark. Jess, studying the trail they were following in the fading light, saw that it was less than three hours old. They had halved the distance between the killers and themselves. They could catch them tomorrow, with a little luck.

He let himself think what it would he like, lying on a rise above the killers' camp, shooting down into them, killing them one by one. He shook his head angrily to clear those foolish thoughts from it. A man and a boy don't go up against seven hardened killers and expect to win. They might kill one or two. But then they'd die themselves. Those remaining would go on, to kill and kill again. And Edie and the twins would be forever unavenged.

He gathered wood along the banks of the little stream beside which they had camped. Abe unsaddled the horses and picketed them where there was grass and no trees to get tangled in. He returned, took the blankets from behind their saddles, and spread them out. When his father returned with wood, he built the fire. Jess filled the coffeepot and put it on to heat. He slicked some antelope meat into the skillet, and when it was done, put sliced potatoes in to fry in the grease.

They talked little, each thinking, in spite of himself, both of what lay behind and of what lay ahead. When they had eaten, Abe washed the dishes and pans out with sand and water, and the two layed down to sleep.

Staring at the starry sky, Jess wondered what thoughts were in Abe's mind.

He couldn't know. Perhaps he would never know. He assumed Abe's thoughts were the same as his. Yet, how could they be? Abe had been Edie's son. He had been her husband.

He closed his eyes. It was a long time before he slept, but finally, near midnight, he dropped off. His dreams were mixed up and horrible. When he awoke, he was bathed with sweat, and there was a harsh, wordless cry upon his lips. Abe was sitting up, having been awakened by his cry. He said, "What's the matter, Pa?"

Jess said, "Nothing. Go back to sleep." He lay there staring at the stars for a while, until he heard Abe's breathing became regular. Then he threw back his blankets and got up. He pulled on his boots and walked out away from camp. His dream was still vivid, and it turned him cold. He had been tied and had been forced to watch while man after man raped Edie as she cried out piteously to him for help. Yet no matter how he strained at his bonds, he could not break free, and in the end the seven men stood in a circle around him, looking down, mocking him and laughing and telling him his wife was dead.

Small wonder he had awakened in a sweat. He walked slowly back to camp, but he was afraid to lie down and sleep again. Afraid, lest such a dream return.

He built up the fire and put some coffee on, and sat staring into the flames until the sky in the cast turned light. He called Abe, then, and by the time the boy was dressed, Jess had breakfast ready—once more antelope meat and potatoes fried in the grease.

They ate, cleaned the dishes with sand, then mounted and rode out. They were still in country familiar to Jess at midmorning when he sighted a lift of dust ahead.

Abe didn't see it, and Jess did not point it out. Once, from the top of a bluff, he was able to make out tiny dots at the foot of the column of dust. He could count only six, but he supposed that was because distance made the figures blur, because two sometimes seemed like one.

Seeing them, knowing they were the ones who had so brutally murdered his family, made him want to hurry and catch them more than he had ever wanted anything. But he knew nothing would be gained by giving way to his feelings. They still were seven, and he and Abe made only two. He wasn't even sure Abe could kill a man when the need for it arrived.

So he clenched his fists and maintained the same distance behind the men, taking care to stay in low ground, careful not to let himself and Abe be skylined so that they could be seen.

Deliberately he dropped back in late afternoon, and

when he made camp, it was in a depression where his campfire would be invisible. He was tired, both physically and in his mind, but when he lay down, he was still afraid to sleep for fear he would have the same dream he had had last night. Eventually, however, he did sleep, and it was a deep and dreamless sleep from which he awoke refreshed.

They rode out before sunup, with Jess squinting into the distance ahead, looking for their prey. It was early afternoon, however, before he once more spotted that lift of dust. Having done so, he stopped to rest the horses, preferring not to take the chance that Abe might see it too.

So far back were they that they did not hear shots. But in late afternoon, they reached a small ranch that the seven had attacked.

A man, perhaps sixty-five, lay dead in the yard, his hands still closed around the stock of his ancient muzzle-loading rifle. He had been literally riddled with bullets and lay in a pool of his own clotted blood. His wife lay dead between him and the house, no marks or visible wounds on her. She had apparently died trying to get to him, of shock, or heart seizure, or fear. The inside of the house had been torn apart by the seven men, who had been looking for money the old couple might have hidden away.

Jess dismounted. He got a shovel from the shed, went a little ways from the shack, and began to dig. Abe was white-faced as he watched, and he finally got up enough courage to say, "We got to get 'em, Pa. Before they do anything else like this."

Jess was thinking that if he had kept going, if he had pressed the seven a little by letting himself be seen, this man and his wife might still be alive. But he hadn't, and now it was too late.

He dug down only about three feet, deep enough so that the bodies would not be disturbed by wolves. He wrapped them, put them in the graves, and covered them. He put no markers on the graves, since he did not know their names. When he finished, it was still light enough to scout around for tracks.

As before, he found the tracks of the seven men and his own buggy horse coming into the yard, later found them leaving it. But he found something else that made his heart pound faster with excitement. He found a spot of blood, and farther on another one, and then, where the wounded man had been helped to mount, another one as big as the palm of his hand.

He called to Abe. He pointed to the spot of blood. "The old man hit one of them."

Abe didn't say anything. Jess was torn between elation that one of the seven was wounded and fear that the man might die before they had a chance to wreak their vengeance on him. He said, "Let's go."

He put his horse into a lope, and Abe kept pace forty or fifty yards behind. Jess stayed with the trail at a steady lope for almost an hour before it got too dark to see.

His horse and Abe's were lathered from the pace. Jess unsaddled and rubbed his horse down with the saddle blanket. Abe dutifully followed suit. Jess built a fire, and they ate, and afterward he said to Abe, "I'm going on. I want you to stay here the night and pick up the trail tomorrow. If I should lose it in the dark, we won't have to come back here to pick it up."

Abe looked scared. "What if I can't find you again?"

"Don't worry about that. I'll find you. If I don't find you by the middle of the afternoon tomorrow, you build a fire and throw a lot of green brush on it so's it'll make a lot of smoke."

"Why can't we both go on?"

"Because we can't be sure those men are going to keep going in the same direction."

Abe nodded reluctantly. Jess gripped his shoulder briefly, then got his horse and saddled and mounted him. He said nothing further to Abe, but rode out, leaving his son standing there looking scared but stubbornly unwilling to admit that be was afraid.

Jess felt briefly proud of him, and then put his mind on the task that lay ahead. He had lost a lot of time burying the old man and his wife. Now he meant to make it up. He wanted that wounded man before he died.

CHAPTER 3

HE PICKED A STAR TO GUIDE HIMSELF, EVEN THOUGH he knew it would shift as the night wore on. He also knew that he had no other choice. No landmarks were visible.

He pushed hard from the start. He was grim and purposeful, like a wolf on the trail of prey. He held his horse to a steady trot, discovering he was glad Abe was not along. He would not be hampered by worry about Abe's safety. He would not have to account to Abe for what he did when he caught up with the wounded man.

And now he made himself think of Edie. He made himself remember what she had looked like on their wedding day, clad from head to foot in white, with a wispy veil covering her face. He remembered what it had been like holding her close to him in the night. He remembered her when she was carrying Abe, and later the twins, and the happy and contented look that her face had worn.

Then, deliberately, be made himself remember what she had looked like staked out on the ground, soiled and ravaged and dead. And that familiar coldness came to his heart, and he knew he could do whatever must be done when the time came for it, unhampered by any code learned long ago before this terrible thing happened to him.

Gradually, as he rode, he shifted course toward the left, still keeping his eyes on the star he had selected earlier, to compensate for its journey across the sky from east to west. Dawn grayed the eastern sky, and he saw a bluff rising ahead, and loped his horse to its foot and climbed it, hopeful that from its top he could spot the breakfast fire the killers would almost certainly have built. They had no inkling anybody was following them. But they would know before very long. Jess meant to make sure of that. They would learn to fear him before, one by one, they died.

He dismounted at the top of the bluff. He squatted like an Indian at its edge, and with narrowed eyes peered out across the undulating plain. He saw nothing for a long, long time, but he was patient and did not strain his eyes. If there was smoke, he'd see it eventually, but not if he forced himself or grew panicky.

When he saw it, he could almost believe he had imagined it. Only a small and bluish spot it was, three miles away. But as be watched, it shifted, and finally it made a tiny column rising in the air, unmistakable at last.

He did not move immediately, but instead studied the lay of the land between him and the tiny column of smoke. He picked a route for himself in depressions and draws, and when he had, he rose and mounted and put his horse down through the steep and rocky rim. He slid the horse down to level prairie and then took the route he had previously selected for himself, alternately walking and trotting the horse. Once he withdrew his rifle from the saddle boot and checked its loads. Having done that, he checked the loads in his revolver and replaced it in the holster at his side.

His route took him to within a quarter-mile of the smoke, which still rose in a thin column toward the sky. Here he found an arroyo perhaps eight feet deep and fifteen feet wide. Brush and scrubby trees grew in the bottom. The arroyo ran at right angles to the direction he wished to go, but it would hide his horse.

He dismounted and tied the horse and withdrew the rifle from the boot. He climbed out of the arroyo and headed toward the smoke, as slowly and cautiously as any stalking Indian brave. Yet despite his caution and seeming coldness, there was a storm raging in him as he thought how close he was to the murderers of his family. He wanted to break into a run. He wanted to rage into their camp and kill and kill until nothing was left alive.

The camp was on an open flat perhaps a hundred yards across. There was little cover closer than three hundred yards. Jess lay behind a clump of sagebrush and stared into the camp.

Nothing moved. Only one horse was visible on the far side of camp, this one saddled and tied to a clump of brush. He could see the fire, and the lumped shape of a man beside it, but he couldn't see any sign of the other six.

Caution rang a steady warning bell in his mind.

Maybe they knew they were being pursued. Maybe they had laid a trap.

Impatience grew in him. Reason told him they had abandoned their wounded companion, left him to die. Slowly he got to his feet and carefully stared around. Still wary, he made a circle of the camp.

On the far side he picked up the tracks of six horses leaving it. He stared in the direction they had gone. There appeared to be no cover capable of hiding six horses and six men for at least a mile.

Turning, he went back into the camp. He walked to within a dozen feet of the figure on the ground. The man's eyes were closed. For an instant Jess thought that he was dead. Then he saw the shallow rise and fall of his chest and knew he was alive.

Cautious still, in spite of the fury growing in him, in spite of his increasing shortness of breath and the trembling of his hands and knees, he stared around. Nothing moved.

He looked down at the man again, at the bearded, dirty face, drawn and greenish now with pain and loss of blood. He thought of Edie and he knew that simply killing this man was not going to be enough. Not to still the grief that tore through him every time he remembered the way they had left his wife. Not to satisfy the thirst for vengeance that was so much worse than any other thirst could be.

Stepping close, he kicked the man savagely in the belly. The man cried out, and opened his eyes. He looked up, pain and comprehension mingling in them. Jess said harshly, "So you've guessed. You're right, you son-of-a-bitch! I'm the husband of the woman you left staked out on the ground."

Fear came to the eyes of the man on the ground. He

licked his cracked and blackened lips and croaked, "I didn't have nothin' to do with it, mister. I told them . . . By God, I tried to stop them. I swear I did."

"Liar!" Jess spat the word at him.

"What you goin' to do to me?"

"Kill you."

Some of the fear left the man's pain-filled eyes. And Jess understood that the man knew he was going to die. His friends had abandoned him, and he had no hope. He might even feel relieved because death would not come slowly as he had expected it to.

Jess said, "But not before I'm through."

"Through doin' what?"

Jess took out his pocketknife. One blade was six inches long, and sharp enough to shave a man. Kneeling, he slit the mans pants and underwear from ankle to waist, then did the same with the other leg. He opened his shirt similarly, then seized the shreds of the ripped pants, shirt, and underwear from the prostrate man. The man said, with alarmed protest, "Hey! What the hell you doin'?"

Jess looked around. A rope was hung from the saddle of the man's horse where he stood tied fifty feet away. He walked to the horse and took it down. Deliberately, he cut four lengths from it.

He looked around for stakes. There were none, but he remembered that there had been dead wood lying around back where he had tied his horse. He headed for that spot, stopping only when he heard a commotion in back of him. Turning, he saw the wounded man, now naked except for his boots, hobbling toward his horse.

Jess raised his rifle deliberately. He shot the man's horse in the neck and watched him crumple forward to the ground. He turned and went after his stakes. When he returned, the wounded outlaw was lying on the ground beside his horse.

Jess walked to him and kicked him savagely. "Get back to the fire, you son-of-a-bitch!"

"I'm hurt!"

"You got to your horse all right." Jess drew back his foot for another kick, and the man began scrambling away. He was gut shot, Jess saw, and his belly was distended and blue from internal bleeding.

Jess was cold and furious. He was shaking, and his face was white. The man asked, "What you going to do to me?"

Jess got a rock and drove the stakes into the ground. He tied ropes to them and then dragged the wounded outlaw over to them. He tied the man's ankles and wrists to the stakes. The man begged, "For God's sake, you can't leave me here like this."

Jess said furiously, "Don't bring God into this, you dirty, murdering son-of-a-bitch!"

"But you can't leave me here like this!"

"I ain't going to leave you here like this." Knife in hand, he knelt. The man screamed when he was touched, screamed again as the knife slashed away his genitals. Jess laid them on his chest where he could see them, wiped the knife on a clump of grass, and pocketed it.

He stared down at the mutilated man, both shocked at what he had done and surprised that it had been no worse than castrating a calf. The man was sobbing hysterically now, wriggling and trying to dislodge the grisly mess lying on his chest.

Feeling a little sick, but also tilled with a fierce satisfaction, Jess turned to go. The man screeched, "For God's sake, shoot me! Don't leave me here alive!"

Jess said, "Maybe you'll live. Maybe someone will come along and save your hide. But you ain't never going to do no other woman like you done my wife."

Heading toward the arroyo where he had left his horse, he suddenly came face to face with Abe. The boy's horse was lathered from hard traveling. He looked beyond his father at the naked man staked out beside the dying fire. He slid from his horse, his face suddenly sweating and pale. He bent double and vomited, and when he straightened, he grabbed his father's revolver from its holster, ran to the fire, and pumped two bullets into the man before Jess could reach him and snatch the gun away.

Jess was furious. He slapped Abe hard on the side of the face, leaving a red handprint there.

Abe's eyes were sick. Jess raged, "Goddamnit, why'd you do that? You know what he did to your ma?"

Abe stared at him with hurt and scared and defiant eyes. He was trembling from head to foot, as if he had a chill. His voice came out shrill and shaking. He screeched, "Sure I know. But it wasn't nothing you ain't done to her before!"

For an instant Jess was too shocked to move. Then reflex brought his hand swinging savagely around. Once more the flat of it struck the side of Abe's face, this time with a lot more force. The boy was flung sideways, and he crumpled to the ground.

And now hysteria tore at him. Sobs racked his body, and he buried his face helplessly in the dust.

Jess stared down at him. The fury, born so suddenly, was gone. He wanted to go to the boy, but he could not. Coldly he said, "I never done nothing *to* your ma. What I done, I done *with* her, and there's some difference. It's the way you got into the world, boy, and it's the way your twin sisters got here too."

Turning away, he walked to the arroyo where he had left his horse. He mounted and returned. Abe bad disobeyed last night. He had followed instead of staying in camp and taking the outlaws' trail when it got light. But it didn't matter now. The harm was done. Abe had seen what Jess had never intended him to see.

Coldly he looked down at his son. Coldly he said, "Quit blubbering and get up on your horse. We got work to do."

Abe got up and staggered to his horse. He did not look at his father, nor did he look at the dead man staked out on the ground.

CHAPTER 4

THEY TRAVELED IN SILENCE FOR A TIME. THE TRAIL was plain and easily followed. It was Abe who broke the silence first. "How come they just left him, Pa?"

Jess hipped around in the saddle and studied his son's face. It was brown from sun and wind, a clean-hewn, flat-planed face more like his mother's than like Jess's was. But Abe had his father's eyes, grayish blue, and his father's mouth, wide and strong and mostly serious. Jess said, "Men like them ain't got any loyalty. That one back there was shot and couldn't keep up. So they went off and left him to shift for himself. I'm surprised they left him his horse." He was untouched by what he had done, but he could see that Abe was still badly shaken and upset, even though he seemed to want to talk, and by doing so, get back on good terms with his father.

Abe said, "But don't they need each other?"

"The whole ones don't need one that's been shot.

And what a hurt one needs don't count for a damn with them."

"Where do you think they're going, Pa?"

"They're not going. They're running away. That one back there had the marks of irons on his legs."

"Running away from where?"

"Deer Lodge, likely. That's the direction they was coming from."

"What's Deer Lodge, Pa? A prison?"

"Yep. Territorial prison in Montana. They send the bad ones there."

Abe was silent for several moments. Finally he said hesitantly, "Pa?"

"What?"

"Can't we just telegraph Deer Lodge?"

"We could, but it wouldn't do any good. Time they got around to doing something, them six would be long gone."

"Couldn't they telegraph ahead?"

Jess was silent for several minutes. He could feel irritation rising in him. He could still remember the awful horror he had felt at seeing Edie staked out on the ground that way. Animals had killed her, not men. Now he was angry because his son seemed to have no stomach for what they had to do.

Yet, however he felt, and however irritated and angry be was, he had to admit that with Abe it was different than it was with him. Until two days ago Abe had never seen a person dead. Seeing his mother staked out like that must have put scars on Abe's soul that might never go away. Seeing what his father had done to the wounded man must have been nearly as terrible.

Jess remembered the first dead man be had ever seen. It had been as terrible in its way, he supposed, as the sight of his mother had been for Abe. It was during the war, and the man had been struck by a cannonball. It had torn clear through him, leaving him only a mangled mass of torn flesh and bloody entrails from neck to hips. Jess had been detailed to bury him, and had thrown up three times before the job was done. Or he'd thrown up once and had the dry heaves twice.

After that, he'd seen so much of death that it had finally become commonplace, the way death and blood become commonplace to a man who works in a slaughterhouse. The worst had been Gettysburg, where thousands died trying to come up a gentle slope to take the stone wall at its top. They died, and were mangled, and were trampled then by others, clawing over them, only to die themselves. It had sickened Jess, but he'd kept firing, because if he had not and those men had reached the top, then he himself would have been the one to die.

So the death of the convict who had helped murder his wife and two little girls bad left him untouched except for the satisfaction it gave to him. He said. "Abe you don't have to go along. I ain't going to hold it against you if you don't. Killin's hard to get used to, and some people never do get used to it. I did, during the war. It don't bother me to kill a man like that one back there. It ain't going to bother me to kill the other six."

Abe was tempted. Jess could see he was. Then Abe's mouth firmed out and his eyes met Jess's own. "I'll go."

"All right, then. Only, I don't want to hear no more sass out of you, no matter what I do."

Abe said, "I won't promise that. "You do things like you done back there, and you ain't no better than them convicts are." Abe's face was white, and his eyes were scared, but they didn't waver, and held Jess's glance steadily.

Jess didn't want to leave Abe behind. But neither did he intend to let Abe dictate what he did. He growled, "I'll do what I damn please when I catch up to them."

Abe didn't answer, and Jess supposed it was just as well. He didn't want to quarrel with Abe. Neither did he want to leave him alone in the state of mind he must be in. Being alone and brooding over what had happened might do irreparable damage to the boy.

Staring ahead, Jess suddenly saw a lifting wisp of dust. He veered quickly aside, and headed toward the nearest cover, a patch of high brush and scrub trees in a hollow a quarter-mile away. Abe asked, "What you doing, Pa?"

Jess said, "Somebody's coming. Maybe they heard the shots."

Galloping along behind, Abe said, "That far away?"

Jess shrugged. It wasn't likely, he admitted. Maybe the man had had second thoughts about leaving his hurt companion behind. Or maybe he was only regretting leaving the man's horse, when be would probably die and have no further use for it.

Jess dismounted as soon as they reached the cover of the brush and trees. Abe followed suit. Jess stood beside his horse, staring at the single horseman galloping toward them. He wondered whether the man would notice their trail breaking off, and let his hand drop to touch his revolver grips. He found himself hoping the man did notice and would come to investigate. If he didn't, Jess would follow him as soon as he was sure the man was alone. He'd catch and kill him, and then there would be only five.

The man wasn't looking at the ground. He galloped

past, heading back toward the place he and the others had left the wounded man. Abe was watching his father's face, perhaps guessing his thoughts. Jess was watching the direction from which the man bad come, making sure his companions weren't following.

The man disappeared. Jess felt Abe's glance on his face. He looked at his son, angered because he felt defensive. Abe asked, "What you going to do?"

Jess said, "Kill him. He helped kill your ma. He helped kill the twins."

Abe looked scared and desperate. Jess said, "Don't try to talk me out of it."

Abe said. "Just killin'. Nothing else."

"Killing's too good for him. He didn't give your ma an easy time of it."

Abe said, "Pa . . ."

For the first time, Jess looked, really looked at his son's face. It was white and scared, and there was something in the boy's eyes. He couldn't have said exactly what it was, but it was disturbing. He said angrily, "What am I supposed to do, let him get away? Damn it!"

Abe looked green. He wouldn't meet his father's eyes. Suddenly Jess knew he had to let the man live, for now at least. Abe couldn't stand any more killing. Not until he'd got over the shock of the last one, and of his mother's and two little sisters' deaths. Conceding that, Jess realized that letting the man go might be better than killing him. He would take the story of what he had seen back to the other five. He would tell them about their wounded companion, stripped and staked out, mutilated and dead.

Let them think about that for a while, he thought. Let them wonder about the scourge that was on their trail, and wonder which of them would be next. He smiled at the thought, a grim smile that made Abe ask, "What's the matter?"

Jess said, "I'll let him go."

"Why?" asked Abe suspiciously. "What made you decide on that?"

Jess said, "It ain't a pretty sight back there. Let him go back to his friends and tell them what he saw. It's goin' to get them thinking; I'll guarantee it will."

Abe's face was relieved. After a moment he said, "Pa, call in the law. The law will catch them and make them pay."

"How?" Jess asked bitterly. "A local sheriff won't go out of his county. The nearest U.S. marshal is likely two hundred miles away, in Denver or in Dodge."

Abe said, "We could follow them until we got someplace where there was a U.S. marshal."

Jess said, "And what could we prove? They're six against two. We couldn't even prove a crime was committed, much less that they committed it."

"Pa, there's got to be a way!"

"There is. And we're taking it. If you ain't got the stomach for it, boy, then you just go on back. Stay with the Robinsons or the Claybanks until I get back."

"One man can't fight six."

"I don't aim to fight them. I aim to kill them, one by one. I can use some help, but by Jesus, I ain't going to argue with you about it all the time."

So heated had the argument become that neither heard the distant hoofbeats approaching them. Jess caught movement out of the corner of his eye and whispered harshly, "Shut up!"

He saw the man who had earlier ridden by now headed south. He was raking the sides of his horse almost frantically, bent low over the horse's withers, whipping the horse's rump with the ends of the reins. The horse was running, but even that didn't seem to satisfy the man. Jess grinned. "He seen his friend. Rattled him some, didn't it?"

Abe did not reply. Jess watched until the man was out of sight. A thin haze of dust hung in the air even after the man was gone. Then he turned his glance on Abe. He said, "Make up your mind. What you going to do?"

Abe said, "I loved Ma too. And I loved the twins."

"You're going, then?"

"Yes, sir. I'm going."

"You ain't going to fight me every time I catch up to one of them?"

"No, sir. Long as you don't do nothing like you done back there."

Jess studied him. There was determination in Abe, and he was plainly trying to be strong. Jess nodded and headed for his horse. He didn't know whether he could control himself when he caught up with the next of the killers. He didn't know whether simply killing the man would be enough for him. He would see the killer's face, and then he would see etched upon his memory the sight of his wife lying there . . .

He'd try to satisfy himself with simply killing quickly and going on. But he couldn't promise anything. Neither to Abe nor to himself.

CHAPTER 5

THE GALLOPING OUTLAW HAD HARDLY DISAPPEARED when Jess was in the saddle again, following. Abe came along behind, his expression blank and unreadable. Jess looked back at his son once, and thereafter kept his glance straight ahead. He hoped he wasn't going to have to argue with Abe every time he caught one of the escaped convicts, but he felt no confidence.

They traveled at a steady trot all afternoon, trying to save their horses while at the same time covering a maximum amount of distance. Abe did not speak, nor did Jess. He tried hard to understand his son, yet he could not help feeling disappointed and ashamed of Abe. The boy, even though only fifteen, had seen his mother's ravaged body and the bodies of the twins. Yet, he seemed disposed to forgive the killers. Or else he had no stomach for what had to be done to them. Either way, he gave Jess little cause for pride.

In midafternoon they struck the camp the killers had made the night before. Jess wasted little time looking around. He saw the galloping prints of the horse ridden by the man they had seen. That trail went straight through the camp, without slackening pace. Jess smiled grimly to himself. The man was badly scared. He wanted to rejoin his companions as quickly as he could. Jess could imagine him looking back a hundred times, searching his back trail for the scourge that had visited such terrible retribution upon the wounded man.

He was glad, now, that Abe had kept him from killing him. He didn't want the remaining six to die easily. They had made Edie suffer before she died. He wanted them to suffer too, not only physically when he caught them, but in their minds. He wanted them to think about their companion staked out naked in the sun, his genitals lying bloody on his chest where he could look at them. He wanted them to think about the possibility that the same fate might befall them too.

He and Abe made a silent camp that night in a little,

watered draw. They were south, now, of the Wyoming-Colorado line, having passed well east of Cheyenne. Abe gathered dry firewood, and Jess built a small fire. They still had potatoes and lard and some antelope meat. Jess knew he ought to start looking for game tomorrow. If he could kill an antelope without losing too much time, he'd be wise to do so. It might save a long detour later, because it was a certainty the six escaped convicts weren't going to leave any food for their pursuers if they could avoid doing so. They'd strip every ranch house they encountered of everything that was edible.

On the following night, Jess did not stop at nightfall, but kept going. The convicts' trail had not deviated for fifty miles. South and east it went, and he felt that he could afford to take the chance that it would continue to. The six escaped convicts plainly had a specific destination in mind and were headed straight toward it.

He wasn't surprised, but be was pleased when, near ten o'clock, he sighted the flickering of a campfire straight ahead. He continued riding toward it, but a quarter-mile away he stopped. Abe asked nervously, "What you going to do?"

"See if I can catch one of 'em alone."

Abe did not reply. Jess rode on cautiously. He wanted to be neither upwind of the convicts' camp, where their horses could smell his and Abe's, nor downwind, where his horse and Abe's could smell theirs. He circled, therefore, until he could come in crosswind. He'd have to hope the wind did not shift. But if he had to make a run for it, darkness would favor him and Abe.

He rode close enough to the outlaws' camp to count them. There were six. One was a huge man, who must have stood six-foot-four. One was the other extreme, thin and slight, and no more than five feet tall. The remaining four were average, neither tall nor short, neither heavy nor overly thin. All were dirty. All were dressed in clothes obviously stolen from ranch houses they had raided along the way. Jess recognized his own jacket at the same time Abe exclaimed, “Pa, one of them is wearing your coat!”

If he had needed proof that these were the guilty ones, he had it now. Their fire was low, mostly coals, and as he watched, one of the men piled the remaining firewood on it and headed away from camp to gather more. Jess headed in the direction the man had gone, and he flung over his shoulder the words, “Abe, take your horse back a half-mile and wait for me.” He yanked his rifle out of the boot. Carrying it, he urged his horse into a trot, trying to get ahead of the man who had left camp looking for wood. Maybe he’d get no chance at the man. Maybe the man would stay too close to camp. But he’d be ready if the opportunity came. He’d be ready, and he’d be free of Abe’s interference, because Abe would be a half-mile away.

He traveled at a trot for about an eighth of a mile, then cut sharply to the right to intercept. Listening, he finally heard a branch crack sharply ahead of him.

Fierce exultation surged through him. Holding his hand over the rifle’s receiver to muffle the noise of the action opening and closing, he jacked a cartridge in. He didn’t want to use the gun, because it would bring the others at a run. But he knew he might need the gun to save his life, because it was certain that by now the convicts were all edgy and ready to shoot the instant any threat appeared.

His horse’s hoof snapped a twig, and for an instant he stiffened, listening. But the branch cracking went on ahead, as the outlaw continued to break dead limbs from the scrubby trees.

Black it was, but there was light enough from the stars to avoid obstacles. And finally Jess saw the man ahead of him.

The man was neither big nor small, being one of the average ones. He had his left arm piled high with branches. He continued to break off more with his right. Jess dismounted and came up on him swiftly from behind, like a wolf leaping upon his prey, and struck him with his shoulder squarely in the small of the back.

A grunt, part from the blow and part surprise, was driven from the man. Then Jess was on him, left hand encircling the man's neck, while his right groped for the outlaw's right hand, which was trying to get out his holstered gun. He got the man's wrist, yanked back the arm, and forced it high against the man's shoulder-blades, so that he cried out with pain.

The outlaw struggled frantically, for he knew who his adversary was. The same one who had mutilated his companion. Jess tightened the arm that encircled the man's neck. He cut off the air flowing in and out of the man's lungs. Desperately the man kicked back at his shins, connecting but not forcing Jess to slacken or release his grip. Inexorably, Jess tightened that arm and held the man until the man's struggles weakened. Still he did not loosen his grip. He waited until the man went limp, and sagged, and only then did he release him and let him collapse to the ground.

First, he stooped and relieved the man of his holstered gun. He flung it away into the darkness and heard its sound as it hit the ground in beavy brush. Then he went to his horse, hurrying. When the man did not immediately return, his companions would come looking for him. Jess wanted to be finished by the time they did.

He got his rope off the saddle. He approached the man, only a dark, lumped shape in the night. Stooping, he put the loop over the man's ankles and tightened it. Rising, he threw the rope over the branch of a tree. Leaving it hang, he went to his horse. He led the animal back, then secured the end of the rope to the saddle by taking three turns around the horn.

Mounting, he kicked the horse in the ribs. The animal balked when he felt the weight, but Jess's steady urging made him move away, raising the outlaw upside down until his head was three feet clear of the ground.

Jess halted his horse. Dismounting, he unwrapped the rope from the saddlehorn. Holding it by bringing the rope around behind him and leaning heavily against it, he went to the trunk of the tree and wrapped it around a couple of times before knotting it. He would be leaving his rope, but it would be worth it. He could get another one.

Now he drew his pocketknife and opened the blade. The man was coming to, and Jess waited, wanting him to be fully conscious before he began. The man began to struggle, but to no avail. His hands could not even touch the ground. Jess said, "Yell, and I'll cut your throat."

The man's yell died in his throat. He choked because of his inverted position, and finally got out, "Who are you, and what are you going to do?"

Jess said, "I'm the husband of the woman you staked out and killed back there a ways. You try guessing what I'm going to do."

"I'll yell. My friends can get here before . . ." The man stopped.

Jess said, "They can't get to you while you're still a

man."

The man said, "For the love of God . . ."

Jess said harshly, "Don't bring God into this."

Behind him, Jess heard a branch crack. He whirled, ready to fire the instant he had anything to fire at. He heard Abe's voice, scared but determined, "Pa . . ."

Furiously Jess said, "What the hell are you doing here?"

Abe didn't answer him. He rode his horse in close. Even in the starlight, he could see the man dangling head down from Jess's rope. He must have seen the gleam of the knife in Jess's hand, because he said, "No, Pa. Not again."

Jess said, "You get out of here. I told you to stay back there."

Abe didn't argue. He didn't say anything. He just dug spurs savagely into his horse's sides.

The startled, frightened animal jumped, dug in, and broke into a gallop. Abe reined him straight at Jess, who jumped frantically, trying to get out of the way.

He was slow, too slow. The horse's shoulder struck him with force enough to throw him fifteen feet and knock him off his feet. It also knocked the breath out of him. For an instant he lay there on his back, gasping, trying to draw air into his lungs.

Abe left his horse running, and the animal stopped, trembling. Abe knelt beside his father and withdrew the revolver from its holster at his side. He groped until he found Jess's hand with the knife in it. He took the knife, got up, and ran to the outlaw hanging upside down.

He tried to reach high enough to cut the rope, but he could not. Turning, he ran to the trunk of the tree and cut it there. The man fell, striking the ground with a thump and a gust of expelled air.

Abe started back toward his horse. The outlaw wasted no time getting the rope off his ankles. Rising, he charged after Abe, and struck him from behind. He knocked Abe sprawling, and followed like a wolf, landing on Abe and knocking the wind out of him.

Jess, still gasping for air, fought to his feet. He stumbled toward the grappling pair, knowing Abe's foolishness could cost him his life in the next few seconds if he did not get there first. While he was still six feet away, a gun blasted, its flare orange and wicked in the darkness, but partially killed by the proximity of a body to the muzzle of the gun. Someone cried out with pain and shock, and then Jess hit the pair with his body, groping for the gun, cursing inwardly his inability to see.

The outlaw pulled away and struggled to his feet. Yelling with frantic urgency for help, he plunged away into the brush.

Abe was down on the ground, groaning with pain. Jess said harshly, "Where the hell are you hit?"

"Leg, Pa. I'm sorry."

"Sorry be damned! We got to get out of here!"

Angrily, careless of Abe's pain, he yanked the boy to his feet. He saw the gleam of his gun on the ground and snatched that up too. Then, half-carrying Abe, be headed for the boy's trembling horse. He raised the boy and literally flung him into the saddle. Turning, he ran for his own mount, even as he heard the pound of many running feet approaching through the brush.

He hit the saddle and reined the horse around. He spurred toward Abe. Leaning over, he grabbed the headstall of Abe's bridle. Both horses broke into a gallop.

Guns flared in the darkness behind them. Bullets

clipped twigs from brush nearby and ahead. Then the two were safely away, and Jess was able to release Abe's horse.

Jess couldn't remember ever having been more furious in his life before. If Abe hadn't been hurt, he'd have whipped him within an inch of his life.

But he promised himself one thing. Henceforth, he'd go after the murderers alone. If Abe didn't have the stomach for it, then, by God, he could stay behind.

CHAPTER 6

JESS MAINTAINED A HARD GALLOP FOR FIFTEEN minutes. Then, abruptly, he changed directions and galloped for fifteen more. He knew Abe was bleeding, and he knew he had to take care of his son's wound. But caring for Abe's wound would be meaningless if the outlaws were permitted to catch up with them.

At last he rode down into a depression ringed with sagebrush and yanked his horse to a halt. He slid from the saddle, tied his own horse and Abe's to clumps of brush. He caught Abe as the boy fell from the saddle, surprised that Abe had not fallen long before this.

He'd need a fire. He said, "Hang on," and began hurriedly to gather wood. There wasn't much. A few dry, dead sticks of sagebrush, which didn't burn readily, but it was all there was, and he'd have to make it do. His knife was gone—lost back there where Abe had cut the outlaw down—so he couldn't shave the wood.

He finally got the fire going enough to give him a little light. He ripped Abe's pants leg to the thigh and exposed the wound. Abe's pants were soggy and sticky with blood. The boy was pale and near to unconsciousness. Jess asked, “Does it hurt pretty bad?”

“It hurts like hell. I’m sorry, Pa.”

Jess ignored that. He had been angry when Abe galloped up, angrier when Abe knocked him down and cut the killer loose. He was still angry, because he knew the man had gone back to his companions and had told them only a man and a boy were pursuing them, husband and son of the woman they’d killed several days before. No scourge was on their trail, no superhuman being to inspire terror in them. Only a man, and now a wounded boy.

It cut Jess’s advantage. It cut his effectiveness and his chance of avenging his family against the remaining six. The wound in Abe’s leg was bad. The bullet had entered his thigh, making a clean, round, bluish hole. Where it had exited was something else. It had torn a ragged hole nearly two inches across. First thing Jess did was check the bleeding. Relief touched him when he saw it was coming steadily and not in spurts. Furthermore, the blood was dark, and not bright red as it would have been coming from a severed artery.

He went to his saddle. The only cloth he had was his blanket. He untied the blanket roll and tore some strips from his single blanket. He made a pad, laid it on the exit wound, which was bleeding the worst, then bound it to Abe’s leg with the strips he had torn. He ripped the end of the bandage, reversed one end, then tied the bandage securely in place. Abe, still conscious, asked weakly, “What are we going to do?”

“Well, you’re not going on, if that’s what you mean. I’ll have to find a town or a ranch where I can leave you and where you’ll get some care. Then I’ll go on.”

“I didn’t mean—”

Jess said harshly, “I don’t give a damn what you

meant. Your ma and your twin sisters were murdered by that bunch of animals. I intend to make them pay for it, and I don't intend to make their dying easy—not a damn bit easier than they made hers. I'm sorry you're hurt, but I'm damn glad I won't have to put up with you anymore."

He could see Abe's face in the firelight. He was briefly sorry for his brutal directness, but he didn't say so. Abe's eyes remained stricken in his almost bloodless face. Jess said, "Do you think you can ride?"

His voice stubborn but very weak, Abe said, "I'll ride all right."

"Good. I'll get the horses and help you mount."

He went to where he had tied the horses. He untied them and returned, leading them. He helped Abe to his feet and boosted him on his horse. He heard Abe's sharply indrawn breath, and heard his harsh, ragged breathing once he was on his horse. He saw the gleam of sweat on Abe's forehead, and he had to admire the way Abe had choked back any cry of pain he might have made.

He scattered the fire and mounted his own horse. He asked, "Want me to lead your horse?"

Abe said, "I'll manage." There was defiance in his voice.

Jess said angrily, "Manage, then," and kicked his horse deliberately into a trot.

Abe's horse came along behind, matching the trot of Jess's mount. Abe jolted up and down helplessly for several moments before he weakly called, "Pa?"

Jess turned his head. "What?"

"Pa, it hurts. Couldn't we let the horses walk?" There was so much pain in Abe's voice that Jess felt instantly ashamed. He pulled his horse back to a walk.

But still he did not relent. He felt balked and furious that he had lost the man he had meant to kill tonight. He felt further irritated because now the killers knew exactly what they were up against and knew that it wasn't much. Besides that, a lot of time was going to be lost before be would be able to return once more to the pursuit. It was even possible that the six would get clear away. A heavy rain would wipe out the trail.

Forcing himself to exhibit a patience he did not feel, he sat his plodding horse until dawn grayed the eastern sky. He was traveling west now, away from the place where Abe had been shot last night. If there were settlements here in the eastern part of Colorado, they'd be westward toward the peaks of the Continental Divide.

When the sun came up, he stopped at a wide, dry, sandy stream bed. He removed the horses' saddles and picketed them. He dug down in the stream bed with his hands until water seeped up and filled the hole.

He built a fire and put some antelope meat on to fry. While it cooked, he looked at Abe's leg, and afterward at his face.

Abe was paying, and paying heavily, for his foolishness last night. Jess gripped his shoulder with a friendly hand and said, "Hang on. We'll find a place where you can go to bed."

"Pa, you could get the law . . ."

Jess said angrily, "Oh, I could, could I? And where could I get the law? You think if I stood up and yelled for them, they'd come?"

He went to the fire and turned the meat. He paced back and forth impatiently, wondering how long it was going to take, finding a place where Abe could stay.

When the meat was done, he took it out of the pan,

added lard, and sliced the last of the potatoes into the grease. Abe said weakly, "I don't know if I can eat."

"You eat. It's the only way you're going to get back your strength."

When the potatoes were done, he fixed a plate for Abe and one for himself. He poured two tin cups full of coffee. He took Abe's food to him and began to eat himself.

Abe tried, but he wasn't able to get much food down. To avoid wasting it, Jess ate what he left. Then he scoured the dishes out and repacked them. He helped Abe to his saddle and set out again. The land stretched away ahead, nearly flat. The mountains weren't visible and wouldn't be until they got within a hundred miles of them. Jess hoped they wouldn't have to travel that far. It scared him to think of the killers getting away from him.

At noon, they still had not sighted anything, but shortly thereafter, they spotted a small bunch of cattle, and not long after that, a narrow, two-track road. Jess stopped, looking to right and left, trying to decide which way to go. There were no tracks in the road, and he knew that whichever way he went, he could as easily be wrong as right. But south was the direction the killers were traveling, so he turned south. Once in a while he looked back at Abe. The boy was obviously in great pain, but he was holding onto the saddlehorn, not complaining or making any sound.

Jess felt a little sorry for him. Abe had made a serious mistake, but he was paying for it.

He was enormously relieved to see a plume of smoke, and as they crested a shallow rise, a soddy up ahead. Besides the sod house, there was a small shed, also built of sod, in back of it, and a frame outhouse about a hundred feet behind the house.

A girl was hanging clothes to a clothesline stretched between the soddy and the shed. She looked up, saw them, gave up what she was doing, and hurried to the house. Immediately a man came to the door, a rifle in his hands.

Jess rode down the shallow slope. He could see the girl standing behind the man, who was white-haired and seamed of face. Jess said, "Howdy."

The old man nodded shortly, giving him no encouragement. Jess said, "Name's Jess Hawkins. This here is my son, Abe."

The old man said, "Jake Donovan. Jennie's my granddaughter."

Jess said, "Abe's been shot. I'd be beholden to you if you could care for him until he can get about again."

"How'd he git shot?"

Jess said, "It's a long story."

Donovan said, "We got time."

Jess nodded. He couldn't blame them much for being wary. He said, "We got a place up north a couple hundred miles. Me and Abe was out greasing windmills a week or so ago, and while we was gone, seven convicts, out of Deer Lodge, I figure, killed my wife and two little girls." He heard his voice saying the words, but it was like someone else was speaking so dispassionately about something that still cut him like a knife. He went on, "They jumped another ranch a little farther on and killed two old people there, but one of 'em got shot in the fracas, and before long they left him behind, because he couldn't keep up with them. We found him."

The old man said, "What'd you do with him?"

"Killed him," Jess said shortly.

"Them convicts—where are they now?"

"South. South and east by maybe thirty miles."

"They ain't coming thisaway?"

Jess shook his head.

"How'd the boy git hurt?"

"We caught up with them again. Caught one of them out gathering wood. I roped him and strung him up by the feet. Abe didn't like what I was fixing to do to him and butted in. He cut the man down, and the man got a gun and shot him in the leg before he got away."

The old man fixed his glance on Abe. Finally he nodded. "He kin stay." He turned his head. "Girl, fix him a bed out in the shed. He'll be well afore winter comes."

"Yes, Grandpa." She disappeared, and reappeared a little later with her arms loaded with blankets. She hurried to the shed, eyes downcast, face pink. Jess dismounted and helped Abe down. With Abe's arm around his neck, he helped him to the shed. Donovan followed.

The girl had fixed a bed on the bare dirt floor. The shed was used for storage. It was dusty, and there were cobwebs around. She said breathlessly, "I'll clean up, soon's I git the chance."

Jess turned to Donovan, after having lowered Abe carefully to the bed. He said, "I ain't got money. They took everything we had. But I'll pay somehow. I'll work it out if I can't do it no other way."

Donovan nodded, neither accepting nor declining. Jess looked down at Abe. He said, "Take care, son. I'll be back soon's I can."

Abe's face was white with pain. He nodded. "Good-bye, Pa."

"Good-bye." Jess could tell Abe didn't think he was ever going to see his father again. And maybe he was not. There still were six vicious, desperate men ahead of him. It would be a miracle if he was able to kill them all before he was killed himself.

He mounted. Donovan and the girl stood beside the doorway to the shed. He raised a hand and waved as he rode away. The girl waved in reply, but Donovan did not. Jess did not look back as he rode over the rise. He put his horse into a gallop. If he did not come back, Abe at least had a horse. He would be able to return to their home and take up where he had left off. Abe would be all right.

And it was a relief to be rid of him. Now Jess could put his whole attention on what he had to do. He'd get no interference from anyone.

He pushed his horse as hard as he dared all the rest of the day, but it was sundown before he reached the place where Abe had been shot the night before. He'd lost twenty-four hours. It might be days before he caught up with the six again.

CHAPTER 7

ABE DID NOT SEE HIS FATHER RIDE AWAY. SO WEAK was he that he almost instantly fell asleep. He did not awake for a full twenty-four hours, during which time Jennie Donovan looked in at him at least fifty times. Finally, in early morning of the day following, he opened his eyes, immediately aware of the fiery pain in his leg, also of the urgent need to get to the outhouse before it was too late.

He sat up. There was a pole in the center of the shed, and crawling to this, he used it to raise himself. He was still fully dressed except that the leg of his pants where his father had torn it flapped loosely as he hobbled out into the morning sun. Jennie, who had apparently been watching, saw him come out and hurried toward him. He growled, "I got to go to the outhouse," and limped toward it, nearly falling each time he put his weight on his wounded leg.

Jennie stood there uncertainly, wanting to help him but embarrassed too. Abe reached the outhouse and went inside, closing the door behind him. He emerged a few moments later, knowing he had reopened his wound, because he felt the warm wetness of fresh blood beneath the bandage. Jennie met him and positioned herself on his hurt side so that he could put his weight on her. He put an arm across her shoulders and saw her face turn scarlet, saw too the way she carefully avoided looking at him.

He was embarrassed himself to be accepting help from her, but he needed it. His face was shining with sweat, and his whole body was bathed with it. They made it back to the shed, and he sank weakly to the bed. Jennie said, "You can't . . . I mean, there's a chamber pot in the house. I'll bring it out to you."

It humiliated him to think of her emptying it, and he said harshly, "Don't need it. I can manage."

Anger touched her voice. "Sure. You can manage. And I'll bet your leg is bleeding all over again. Isn't it?"

"What if it is?"

"Well, that'll mean it'll be just that much longer before you're well."

"And before I can leave. Is that what you're trying to say?"

"No, it wasn't."

He said stiffly, "I'm sorry to be a trouble to you. I'll be gone in a couple of days."

Jennie looked at him helplessly. He was hurt, and she wanted to help him, but he was as fiercely independent as a wounded hawk she had once brought home. He'd chafe at his helplessness, just as the hawk had, until he was able to leave again. Moreover, he'd reject fiercely every friendly overture, grudgingly accepting only what he had to have.

She asked angrily, "And what will you do when you do get well? Catch up with your father? How do you think you're going to do that? His trail will be gone."

"I'll find him. Don't you worry about that."

Hands on hips, she stared down at him furiously. Then, as if trying to avoid saying what she wanted to say, she turned and went out, slamming the shed door so hard that dust sifted down from the sod roof.

Abe was as angry as she, but he also knew he had been wrong. Jennie and her grandfather hadn't had to take him in. He owed them for doing so. The least he could do to repay that debt was to be agreeable.

He closed his eyes. If only he hadn't interfered the other night when his father had hoisted the escaped convict by the heels and approached him with his knife. But he'd known what his father meant to do, and he had acted instinctively to stop it.

Maybe he had been wrong. Maybe the outlaws deserved what his father had in mind for them.

But he couldn't accept that idea. Just because the seven escaped convicts had been animalistic murderers didn't mean he and his father had to turn into the same thing.

He thought about what Jennie had said about the trail being gone. The more he thought about it, the more desperate he felt. Finally, overcoming his weakness by sheer force of will, he sat up and reached for his boots.

He got them on after much tugging. He thought he was going to pass out pulling the boot on his wounded leg, but he did not. With his boots on, he crawled to the center posts and pulled himself upright again.

His saddle was lying on the floor beside the door. The bridle and blanket were draped over it. He picked up saddle, blanket, and bridle and stepped out the door.

The first time he put his weight on his wounded leg, it collapsed under him. He lay there, head reeling, for a moment. Then he crawled toward the wall of the shed so that he could use it to pull himself erect again.

Jennie reached him before he could reach the wall. Her face was white, and her eyes were furious. "What do you think you're doing?"

"Leavin'," he said in a surly voice. "I don't want to be a burden to you."

For an instant she stared down at him, hands on hips. "Well, I never! You ain't no burden! Nobody ever said you was. Now, you just get back in there and give yourself a chance to mend! You want to die out there before you even find your pa's trail?"

"I won't die. I can make it."

She said, "All right. Make it. Go on and get up. Go saddle your horse. He's right there in the corral. Then get up on him. But don't ask for any help, because I ain't going to give you none."

He glared up at her. He knew he couldn't make it as far as the corral. He knew that even if he did, he couldn't catch and saddle up his horse. Furthermore, he knew that even if the horse was saddled and ready, he couldn't mount.

Jennie saw the defeat come into his eyes. Instantly her challenging attitude was gone. She knelt beside him. "I'm sorry. I didn't mean to talk so hateful to you. But you can't go, and you'd just as well face up to it. You got to stay here until your leg heals up."

Abe was stubborn, but he was not a fool. He nodded. Jennie put her arms around him and helped him up. Leaning heavily on her, he made it back to his bed. He collapsed onto it, and Jennie pulled off his boots as carefully as she could.

Again he slept the clock around. When he awakened on the following day, he was not only ravenous, but felt much better except for the throbbing ache in his leg.

Jennie was there when he awoke, and she immediately went into the house and got him broth and bread, which he wolfed down as though he hadn't eaten for a week. Jennie watched him, and when he had finished, brought him more, which he ate more slowly. She said, "You're better."

He nodded. "Where's your grandpa?"

"Gone. He's gathering steers, getting ready to ship them with a pool herd to Pueblo."

"And he leaves you here alone?"

"What else can he do? Besides, I'll be all right."

"That's what Ma thought."

"I've got a gun."

He didn't pursue the subject any further. The chances were, she *would* be all right. She took the dishes back to the house. Abe got up, and using the crutch Jennie's grandfather had apparently made for him, he hobbled to the outhouse, careful not to reopen his wound. He was sweating a little when he got back, but was otherwise unharmed by the exertion.

He slept again, and awoke, and ate, and slept again. But by the time a week had passed, he was sitting up a good bit of every day, and a lot of the normal color had returned to his face. Jennie changed the bandage regularly, washing the wound with some of her grandfather's whiskey and binding it up again with clean bandages made of flowered cloth that had come from either an old petticoat or a dress.

Abe would sit in the sun in front of the little shed, soaking up the heat, sometimes dozing, sometimes talking to Jennie, who was a good listener. And to her he poured out his confusion over what his father had done to the wounded convict they had caught, over what he had tried to do to the second, whom they had caught gathering wood.

"I reckon they had it coming," he said to her. "Only, treating them that way made us just as bad as them."

"What did your pa do to the one he caught?"

Abe didn't want to say. Jennie said, "You can tell me. I'm not a child."

Abe said, "Well, he stripped him, just like they done Ma. He staked him out on the ground. Then he cut on him with a knife, an' he laid what he cut off on the man's chest where he could look at it."

Jennie's face was white, and she looked as if she were going to be sick. Abe said, "I didn't want to tell you, but you said you wasn't no child."

"And I'm not," she said firmly. "Do you think that's what he meant to do to the second man?"

Abe nodded. "I know it was."

"Then you did right, stopping him."

Abe said, "I ain't so sure. Now I'm here, and he's alone, and maybe they'll kill him instead of him killing them."

"Why didn't he go to the law?"

"He said that even if be could get a lawman on the trail before it got wiped out, the law still wouldn't catch the men, and even if they did, all they'd likely do was send 'em back."

Jennie said, "But that's the reason we got law. To handle things like that."

Abe found himself taking his father's side. "Only Pa was right. We couldn't have got no lawman to go after them. And even if he had caught 'em, he wouldn't have done enough to them to satisfy me an' Pa."

"Then you think your father's doing right?"

He shook his head, a little confused himself. Finally he said, "I reckon killing them men would have been all right. Just killing them. I reckon I could of gone along with that. But not cutting on them with a knife before they died."

She said, "Well, you likely won't find your pa again. Not unless he comes back."

Abe knew that was true, but it was hard to accept. He'd thought he could catch up with his father, but now he accepted the truth. Catching up was impossible. The trail was probably obliterated, and there was only a chance in a thousand of ever finding his father if he did follow him.

Jennie fed him well, and he slept fifteen hours out of every twenty-four. By the middle of the second week, he figured he was about ready to leave. He'd go back home, he thought. He'd take care of the place until his father returned to it.

Sitting out in front of the shed on what he figured was his last day, he stared at Jennie hanging clothes on the line and knew that he didn't want to go. When she reached up to hang something, her dress pulled tight against her hips and outlined her breasts in front. Watching, he felt something stir in him that was strange and new.

And suddenly he understood what had been between

his father and mother, and he understood the difference between that and the violent, forcible rape by the seven escapees from Deer Lodge.

He wanted Jennie, wanted her in bed with him. But be wouldn't hurt her for anything. She turned her head and saw him watching her. She saw the expression in his eyes, and even though it was something new to her, she understood it with the age-old instinct that women have, and her face flushed a painful red. For an instant her glance held his, and then it dropped away. She stopped what she was doing and hurried to the house. She disappeared inside and did not reappear until Abe had gone back into the shed.

Thereafter, their relationship was different. No longer were they girl and boy. Now, suddenly, they were man and woman, and both were aware of it.

And now, for the first time, Abe thoroughly understood his father's fury when he had compared the relationship his father and mother had with the brutal rape committed on her by the outlaws.

He had been a fool, a young and stupid and callow fool. When he saw his father again, he'd tell him so.

If he ever saw his father again. He realized that if his father died at the outlaws' hands, it would be his fault.

Confused and unhappy, he watched Jennie out at the clothesline through the open door as she finished hanging out the clothes. And he wondered bleakly what he was going to do if his father did not come back.

CHAPTER 8

JESS HAWKINS SPENT THE FIRST NIGHT AWAY FROM Abe angrily trying to sleep but succeeding only partially. He couldn't follow trail in the dark, and knew it, but there was a vast impatience in him to be following, to close the distance and make up the time that he had lost.

By his calculations, he was two full days behind. Even if he pushed his horse unmercifully and risked ruining him for good, he couldn't close the two-day gap in less than four. Nor did he dare try traveling at night and hope to pick up the trail again when it got light. It was too risky, and would be doubly hard on his horse.

No. Patience was the only answer, however hard it came. But he was up while the sky still was dark, and as soon as it was light enough to see the ground, he was trailing once again.

Fortunately, it was the dry season of the year. Also fortunately, there were six men ahead of him. Six horses, plus the stolen buggy horse, made a plain and unconcealable trail.

He was able, therefore, to pick his own gait, limited only by his judgment of his horse's remaining strength.

All day he traveled south, trotting his horse half the time, walking him the rest. Too much haste now would only result in the outlaws getting away from him, and he knew this very well.

He discovered that he was glad that Abe was gone. He was glad to be hampered neither by the boy's presence nor by his scruples. Alone, he could do what he liked to the men he caught. He could satisfy in full measure the burning thirst for revenge that still smoldered in his heart. Edie would be avenged. Her murderers would pay in kind for the way they had killed her. Mutilation and slow death would be their fate, accompanied by fear if he could reinstill it in them. The trouble was that they now knew who was pursuing them. And six tough, desperate men are not likely to be intimidated by a single man, no matter how determined he may be, and an adolescent boy.

First, then, he must kill the one who had seen him and who could therefore identify him. He must kill that man quickly and certainly, however he could, to protect his identity.

He trailed that day until it was too dark to see the ground. Again he camped, out of food and hungry. He drank water to fill his belly, but he knew that tomorrow, even if it cost him time, he had to have something to eat. He should have gotten food at the Donovan place, but he had forgotten, being too anxious to be on the trail again.

He slept better this night, his anger having faded somewhat with time. But when he was not asleep, he let himself think of what it would be like once again to have one of the killers beneath his knife.

And sometimes, when he was not thinking these terrible, bitter thoughts, he thought agonizingly of Edie, and of the twins, and of the love that had filled their lives before these escaped convicts from Deer Lodge came to ruin everything.

In the morning, he was on the trail again. He was in southern Colorado now, and in late afternoon swam his horse across the Arkansas. He spotted the fresh trail of a deer in the brushy bottom on the far side, and followed it until, as the sun was setting, he came upon the animal browsing in a little grove of young cottonwood shoots. He fired quickly and saw the young buck fall, and rode to him, his mouth already watering in anticipation. He gutted the animal, hoisted him up, and laid him across his saddle, securing him by cutting a hole in his side between two ribs and pushing the saddlehorn through the hole. He mounted behind the saddle and trotted the horse back to where he had left the trail.

It was nearly dark by the time he reached the place. Dismounting, he hung the deer in a tree, built a fire, and while it got going, skinned the deer's two hindquarters. He hung these in the tree, slashed off several chunks, then spitted them on sticks and put them over the fire to cook.

He staked out his horse while he waited, and refilled his canteen from the Arkansas.

He began to eat ravenously while the meat was still raw inside. By the time he ate the last piece, though, it was cooked just right. He felt gorged and drowsy, but he felt stronger, and he knew that now he would not have to stop again. He had lost no more than a couple or three hours, and he could probably make that up tomorrow. He judged the outlaws' trail was now hardly more than a day old.

He slept well this night, but dreamed a lot and woke occasionally sweating from the awfulness of his dreams. Again at dawn he was on his way, crossing the empty rolling plain and seeing, once, the misty, distant mountains lying to the west.

Sometimes he saw a few cattle, and once a band of horses grazing on a ridge. He debated trying to catch one of them, but gave it up. By stealing a horse, he might invite pursuit by the owner, and that might jeopardize his whole mission. He passed one small ranch house so far away he could hardly make out the buildings, and near dark saw the faint lights of a small settlement in the distance to the west.

The outlaws were stopping nowhere now, not for food, horses, whiskey, or women. He felt a growing satisfaction at that. He'd put fear into them, and even though they knew he was only one, accompanied by a boy who had no stomach for the things he did, they could not altogether conquer their dread of him. Running in a pack like wolves, they were basically cowards, he thought. Individually they had no courage of their own. Their courage was the courage of the pack, which knows nothing can long stand in its way.

Jess was up even earlier on the following morning, anxious because he knew he might overtake his prey today. He cooked himself some more of the venison and then wrapped the remaining, thoroughly chilled meat in his blankets and tied it behind his saddle.

It was hard today not to urge his horse past the point he knew was safe. Hourly the trail seemed fresher, and in late afternoon he found a pile of horse manure that was still warm. He knew, then, that he would catch up with them tonight. He could watch their camp from the darkness and pick out the man who had seen him and could identify him. He could slip into their camp after they were asleep and kill the man before they knew what was going on. Their alertness would be dulled because of the six days that had passed without seeing him.

More cautiously now, he went on. The sky faded and turned dark, and stars winked out. No longer could Jess see the trail, but he had his direction and knew it wouldn't vary much.

An hour after dark, he topped a rounded knoll and

saw a fire about a mile ahead, only a winking orange spot in the night. He neither stopped nor slowed, but he felt a savage exultation. He had caught up with them. He could pick up where he had left off nearly a week ago when Abe had interfered.

He rode to within a quarter-mile of the fire. He tied his horse, knowing this was far enough away so that there would be no exchanging of whinnies between his own horse and those of the outlaws.

He doubted if, after nearly a week, the outlaws would be watching their back trail or posting any guards, but he took no chances. He had six men to kill, one by one. He'd never succeed by being careless or by assuming things he did not know were facts.

Circling, then, he came upon their camp from the east, picking his way slowly and carefully through the knee-high grass. When he had come close enough to recognize the man he had so nearly killed a week ago, he stopped and hunkered down and waited patiently.

The outlaws' horses were dim shapes beyond the fire, staked out and grazing. Two men sat staring into the fire. Three more were stretched out nearby, heads cradled in their hands, staring at the sky. The sixth appeared, coming from the darkness. He threw an armload of buffalo chips upon the fire, and a column of smoke rose from it.

Jess had recognized his man. He was one of those staring into the flames. Jess studied him, memorizing his clothing, his hat, and when he got up, the way he moved. Silent and motionless as an Indian, he waited, and at last the replenished fire began to die. The three men who were lying down went to their saddles and got their blanket rolls. The one who had fed the fire a while back followed suit. And finally, Jess's man also got his blanket roll and lay down to sleep.

Carefully Jess marked his location in his mind. It would be completely dark when he went into the camp, and he didn't want to make any mistakes.

Having satisfied himself as to where the man he wanted had put his bed, Jess got silently to his feet and at a trot returned to where he had left his horse. He mounted and rode back, coming in from the east but checking the wind as he did, to make sure the scent of the outlaws' horses would not be carried to his horse, nor the smell of his horse carried to those of the outlaws. Content that there was little chance of it, he tied his horse to a clump of brush. He took off his boots and put them down beside the clump of brush. He drew the knife he had gotten from Donovan, tested its cutting edge gingerly with his thumb, then moved down toward the camp.

By now the fire was only a bed of glowing coals. At the edge of the camp, Jess stopped, knife in hand, and looked at each of the six outlaws carefully in turn. All appeared to be asleep, but he knew he couldn't count on it. For nearly ten minutes he stood there, and none of the lumped shapes moved. Three of the men were snoring, two softly, one noisily.

There was enough reddish glow in the camp for Jess easily to pick out the shape of the man he meant to kill. And now he moved, swiftly, silently, like a shadow or a stalking panther. He crossed the little clearing. He knelt beside the man he wanted, and clamped a hard, powerful hand over the man's mouth.

The man awoke, and this was what Jess wanted. His eyes looked up, saw Jess, and widened with terror, because he knew death was very close. He tried to struggle. His hands came up to seize Jess's knife hand, but Jess gave him no chance to do it. Swiftly the knife flashed. Deeply it cut. Blood spurted from the doomed man's throat as the knife severed the jugular vein. It made a bubbling sound because of the severed windpipe.

The man knew he was dead. He knew less than a minute of his life remained. He tried to seize Jess, and did, but there was no strength in his hands. He tried to cry out, but his severed windpipe would let no air pass over his vocal cords.

Jess pulled free of the man's clutching hands. The man's blood was on him as he rose to his feet and left the camp as swiftly and as silently as he had entered it. The gurgling continued behind him as the doomed outlaw made it to hands and knees and crawled to the nearest of his companions. He collapsed across the man, waking him, bringing a sudden shout from him.

All was then confusion and hubbub in the outlaw camp, but Jess had already reached his horse. He pulled on his boots, untied the horse, and swung onto his back. Deliberate and slow, he let the horse walk away from the camp, and not until he was an eighth of a mile from it did he kick the horse in the ribs and let him lope.

He felt no remorse over what he had done, only satisfaction. He had waked the man and had let him know he was going to die. The man had recognized him, and had known, in the last minute of his life, what he was dying for.

Two, then, were dead, and five were left. Jess galloped hard for half an hour. Then he swung to the ground, unsaddled his horse, rubbed him down, and staked him out. He took his blanket roll from behind the saddle and lay down to sleep. He slept almost immediately, but it was not a deep sleep, and twice he awakened at some small noise made by bird or rodent near him.

He got up a good hour before dawn, saddled and mounted his horse, and rode out again, heading south and east. When the sun came up, he was lying prone on the top of a timbered ridge, and he saw them coming several miles away.

Surprisingly, they stopped while they were still a couple of miles away. They remained still for five or ten minutes, apparently arguing among themselves. Then they turned and went back in the direction from which they had come.

Jess Hawkins frowned as he got to his feet. He had not expected this. He had expected them to pursue him, and had planned on laying an ambush for them as soon as he found a suitable place.

Now he would have to change his strategy. He would have to go after them again, knowing they might well lay an ambush for him at any time, in any place.

He got his horse and mounted him. He had never expected this to be easy, and it wasn't going to be. With each outlaw that he killed, the others would become more wary and alert.

But kill them all he would. He had promised Edie that.

CHAPTER 9

JESS HAWKINS TRAVELED AS FAST AS HE DARED ON THE trail of the retreating killers. But wherever the land was less than flat, wherever there appeared to be concealment for an ambusher, he slowed or circled, and because of this he was several miles behind the five when they turned and took the trail he had made coming after them. When he caught up and saw what they had done, it was midday.

He halted, frowning. In one way, the outlaws backtracking him gave him an advantage. He knew where he had been and could circle ahead and ambush them. But another aspect of it made a cold fist of ice form in his chest. The end of the trail they were following was the Donovan ranch, where Abe was, where Jennie and her grandfather were. If anything happened to him . . . It gave him chills to think of it.

It was up to him, therefore, to eliminate the men before they could reach Donovan's. He had to kill them all, or they'd kill Abe and Jake Donovan, and they'd treat Jennie the way they'd treated Edie, and leave her dead when they were through with her.

For the first time since taking the vengeance trail, Jess Hawkins had gnawing doubts. What if he failed? What if his horse played out and he fell behind? What if they managed to kill him? They might not stop because they had. They might go on, and kill Abe and Donovan and Jennie out of pure viciousness.

He felt like he was walking a tightrope as he fell in behind them and continued following. He didn't dare fall too far behind. Neither did he dare overtax his horse.

So he contented himself with gaining ground slowly throughout the afternoon. They were still four days away from Donovan's. Maybe the five convicts would give up before they had returned all the way. After all, there must be some pursuit of them by the prison officials at Deer Lodge. Telegrams must have gone out to law-enforcement authorities. The convicts had to get to Mexico quickly if they were going to be safe.

At nightfall Jess still had not sighted the five, but then, he had not dared ride either fast or recklessly, knowing it was still possible for them to ambush him.

They probably would stop, he thought, because they couldn't follow trail in the dark. Admittedly, they were still following their own back trail as well as his, but they had no way of knowing where he had come into it. Besides that, their horses needed rest.

So he kept riding, traveling by landmarks that he remembered instead of following trail. This way he could avoid coming upon them unexpectedly. And if he could get ahead of them, tomorrow he could lay an ambush of his own for them.

What would they expect of him? he asked himself. Well, they would expect him to do exactly what he meant to do. They'd know it scared him to think of them heading back to Donovan's.

And what measures would they take to defeat his ambush? Well, they'd likely put one of their number out to the right, another to the left, as flankers or outriders, hoping to smell out the ambush before they rode into it. Other than that, there was nothing much they could do, except to count on their superior numbers to surround whatever ambush he did set up for them. They wanted to kill him as badly as he wanted to kill them. They knew that as long as he was alive, not one of them was safe.

He saw no winking fires, but then, he had not expected it. He traveled half the night, and finally circled back to the trail. Where it had wound down the steep face of a bluff, he stopped, staring up. They would expect him to conceal himself in the rimrock at the top, he thought. Well, he'd do the unexpected, then. There were rocks, and big ones, at the foot of the bluff, rocks that had broken off the rim in ages past and tumbled down. They were big enough to conceal him, but not his horse. He'd have to hide the horse in an arroyo a quarter-mile away. He'd have to run from rock to rock after he had done as much damage as he could to them, and thus, hopefully, get away.

If they pursued him . . . well, at least they'd no longer be heading toward Donovan's.

He staked his horse out where there was grass, and lay down to sleep. Dawn would be soon enough to hide the animal in the arroyo and to take his own position in the rocks.

He was tense and nervous and had difficulty sleeping. The best he finally managed was a series of short naps, from which he awoke each time with a start. Finally, as gray seeped across the sky, he got up, tightened the cinch on his saddle and coiled the picket rope, then led the horse into the arroyo, where he tied him to a clump of brush. Going back, he stopped fifty yards short of the trail behind a rock that was about four feet high. He could shoot over the top of it, giving them a damned poor target at which to shoot. They would be exposed.

Waiting, his nervousness increased unaccountably. He had a dismaying premonition of disaster. Irritably, he examined the situation, trying to decide what he expected to happen that was so terrible.

If they had flankers out, the one on the left might come between him and his horse. The man might even blunder on the horse, which would leave him afoot and at their mercy. This was what had been troubling him, he thought. This was why he felt the way he did.

Accordingly, he hurried to his horse and led the animal back. If there were no rocks high enough to conceal the horse, then he would have to hide the horse behind what rocks there were. He took down his rope, put the noose around one of his horse's hind feet, then expertly threw the horse to the ground by half-hitching it around his other hind foot and one of his front feet. The horse kicked a little, but finally stopped as Jess soothed him with soft words and a stroking hand.

Now, with the horse concealed, Jess turned to look back along the trail. He saw a lift of dust, which materialized in fifteen minutes into three horsemen. Looking to right and left of them, Jess saw the flankers, out about an eighth of a mile.

He waited, and when the three were a quarter-mile away, saw one of them wave an arm forward, indicating to the flankers that they were to go on ahead and climb the bluff.

Jess breathed a soft sigh of relief. With the flankers on top of the bluff, it would mean he had to face only the three down below. And with his horse close by, be figured he could handle that.

He watched the flankers climb the bluff. The other three halted and waited until they had reached the top. When they had, the three came on.

In Jess the tension had mounted until it was nearly intolerable. He was not blind to the danger of the situation in which he had placed himself. With three men ahead of him, three that could split, and would, and two behind, he was effectively surrounded. It was even possible that when the two flankers got into position after checking out the top of the bluff, they would see him and his horse and signal the others where he was.

He therefore had no time to waste. Surprise was the only thing in his favor, and when that was gone, he'd be foolish not to get out of here as quickly as possible.

He kept his head down until he figured they were less

than a hundred yards away. Cautiously, then, he poked it up. Simultaneously he heard a shout from the top of the bluff. The flankers had seen him. But their words couldn't be understood this far away, and it would be several moments before they could make themselves understood by gestures alone.

The three ahead of him were frozen by the shout from above, staring at the gesturing flankers on the bluff. They hadn't seen him, because they were looking up. He drew a bead on one of the three, aware that the range, which was closer to a hundred and fifty yards than a hundred, was a little long for precise accuracy.

He squeezed off his shot, and heard the bullet hit, and jacked another cartridge in.

But he got no chance to shoot. Already two of them had split off to right and left, galloping. He had to get out, and immediately, or he'd be trapped.

Whirling, he threw off the rope from his horse's feet. The animal came up, frightened and ready to bolt. Holding his rifle, Jess Hawkins vaulted to his back and sank spurs into his sides, hoping the horse had not lost too much circulation from being on the ground.

He pointed the horse straight at the wounded man, who was writhing on the ground, intending to finish him off as he galloped past. But behind him, both men on the bluff opened up with their rifles; and from right and left, the two who had split away from the wounded man also began firing.

A bullet creased his horse's rump, and the animal bowed his back. For an instant Jess thought he was going to buck, and yanked his head up savagely. The horse changed his mind and ran harder instead of bucking. Jess thundered past the wounded man, who tried to reach his gun but failed to get his hands on it in time. A quick glance let Jess know where he had hit his man. There was a spreading spot of blood on the man's shirt front, a mortal wound, he guessed, but one that would not cause death immediately.

Then he was past, and away, and he let his horse run hard for more than a mile. Topping a low knoll, he looked behind.

They had pursued him for half a mile, then had stopped, either to tend their wounded companion, which he doubted, or out of reluctance to wear their horses out chasing him. They were returning toward the bluff.

He let his horse blow. The animal was sweating heavily, and breathing raggedly. He dismounted, loosened the cinch, and squatted. The outlaws stayed only a moment where their wounded companion was. Then they went on, trailing two horses now, the buggy horse stolen from Jess and their wounded companion's horse. Once more they had displayed their callousness and their complete lack of loyalty.

The fact that they were continuing along Jess's back trail confirmed what he had suspected earlier. They were going to Donovan's, knowing he had to try stopping them before they could reach the place. They didn't have to chase him. They knew he must come to them.

Furthermore, he suspected that now they wanted revenge of their own. He had hounded and harassed them, and had decimated their ranks by bringing down three of their number. They wanted to hurt him, and knew that by killing his son they could hurt him most.

The two reached the top of the bluff and joined the two waiting there. The four went on, and disappeared from Jess's view.

He rode back toward the foot of the bluff.

Determinedly, be fought down the growing coldness in his spine. He reached the wounded man, who was still trying to crawl to his gun. Dismounting, Jess picked it up and threw it away. He knew he didn't dare follow the remaining four anymore by trailing them. So it wouldn't matter if he took a little time here.

The wounded outlaw was obviously in great pain. Sweat bathed his face, and his features were twisted with his agony. Jess got his rope. He cut it into four lengths. Then he got four big rocks and positioned them. After that, he knelt and cut the man's clothes off him. The wound was, indeed, in the man's chest. The bullet had apparently pierced his lungs, because a light pinkish froth came from the bullethole every time he breathed. Jess tied a length of rope to each wrist and each ankle, then in turn tied each length to one of the rocks. He looked down at the man staked out naked there, wanting to mutilate him the way he had the first one he'd caught, but thinking instead of Abe. Finally he put his knife away and mounted his horse.

The outlaw knew he was going to die, and this one had too much pride to beg. He just stared at Jess with hating, virulent eyes. Jess rode past and spit straight into his face. Then he headed around the bluff, in some way satisfied with that.

Yet, as he rode, something nagged at him. He felt depressed. He realized when he examined his own feelings that he didn't like himself. He had brought himself down to the outlaws' level by the things he had done to them.

There had been great satisfaction in mutilating the first outlaw. There had been almost as much satisfaction in his cold-blooded murder of the second. But there had been no satisfaction in staking the third man out naked in the sun. Abe had been right. Killing the men who had murdered his wife and the twins was necessary, because there was no way of capturing them and bringing them to trial. But neither torture nor mutilation was. And by indulging in it, he lessened himself and he sinned against the memory of his wife.

All morning he traveled, occasionally seeing the dust of the remaining four outlaws in the distance on his left. No longer could he doubt what they meant to do. He had stung them, hurt them, enraged them. They were going back to Donovan's to kill Abe. They didn't yet know about Donovan and Jennie, but if he didn't stop them, they'd kill them too. In a way both brutal and typical.

CHAPTER 10

IN MIDAFTERNOON JESS HAWKINS HAD NOT GAINED ON the four outlaws traveling a parallel course to the left of him. Their dust was in exactly the same position it had been when he first spotted it. Worry began to trouble him, because he knew he didn't dare force his horse to greater speed. He didn't dare risk exhausting the animal when so much depended on his reaching the Donovan ranch ahead of the four remaining escapees from the prison in Deer Lodge.

Even before the light began to fade from the sky, he had a sinking feeling that he had lost. His horse was nearer exhaustion than he had thought. The animal traveled with his head down, often stumbling, and finally Jess got off and walked.

He didn't know whether the outlaws would camp at dark or not. He did know that if he were to prevent them from going straight to Donovan's, he would either have to give himself up to them or confront them and force a showdown in which he surely would be killed. If things went on as they were, the outlaws would beat him to Donovan's. He would arrive to find his son, Jennie, and Donovan dead. Furthermore, he would lose the outlaws forever, because they would have obtained fresh horses from Donovan.

Accordingly, as soon as dusk grayed the sky, he began to angle left. He kept looking for the winking light of the outlaws' fire, but saw nothing.

Panic now put a cold chill at the base of his spine. For the first time since finding Edie and the twins dead, he began to regret the things that he had done. If he'd been content with simply killing the outlaws one by one, Abe would not have been wounded, and he wouldn't now be facing the problem of their backtracking toward Donovan's. But it was too late for worrying about might-have-beens. The damage was done, and he was faced with the problem of stopping the outlaws before they could reach Donovan's.

He traveled another couple of miles. Then his horse suddenly pulled back on the reins and stopped. Before Jess could do anything, the horse lay down. Over on his side he went, breathing hoarsely and shallowly.

Jess tugged at the reins, trying to get him up, without success. The horse wasn't going any farther tonight. Maybe he'd never get up again.

Nervously Jess paced back and forth. Once he walked to the top of a nearby rise and scanned the horizon in the direction he was headed. He saw nothing. He listened, and heard nothing.

He walked back to his horse. The animal was very silent. Jess bent down and put a hand on the horse's side. The horse was dead.

Now the panic in Jess was greater than it had ever been in his entire life. He was out here alone, and afoot, and he hadn't a chance of overtaking the outlaws. He was three days from Donovan's by horseback. If he had to walk, it would take him more than a week.

Nor did there appear to be any chance of getting another mount. Even if there had been a ranch in the neighborhood, Jess bad no money with which to buy a horse. That wouldn't stop him, of course. If he found a ranch, and a horse was available, he'd take him at gunpoint if there was no other way. But he'd seen no sign of ranches when he rode through here several days ago.

He didn't even consider taking his saddle off the horse. He untied his blanket roll and took his saddlebags, canteen, and rifle, and left everything else.

He began to walk, pacing himself, knowing undue hurry would be self-defeating in the end.

Straining his eyes ahead, he looked for the outlaws' fire. He saw nothing. He kept trying to tell himself that all was not yet lost. The outlaws' horses must be nearly as worn out as his had been. They *had* to camp tonight, even if they didn't build a fire.

But even if they camped, he knew he could go by them in the darkness without knowing it. He could go past a quarter-mile away and hear nothing, see nothing. And he couldn't pick up their trail in the dark. There weren't even any stars to light the ground dimly.

God was punishing him, he thought, for what he had done to the three outlaws he had caught. That phrase in the Bible, "vengeance is mine, saith the Lord," was not a collection of idle words.

Even so, he could not wholly regret what he had

done. He could not have kept from following the killers. He could not have let them get away with such a horrible crime and done nothing. Nor could he have taken it to the law, because there was no law close enough to have been effective in catching and punishing the criminals.

At intervals he stopped and listened, vainly. Finally he decided there was only one thing left for him to do. He must walk as far as he could before he stopped for the night. When he did stop, it must be on a high point of land from which he could see for miles around as soon as it got light. If he walked far enough, and if he stayed reasonably close to the trail, he had a chance of seeing the outlaws when they passed.

Not, he thought bitterly, that it would do him any good. He was still afoot.

So he plodded on north throughout the night, stopping only when the sky turned gray. He picked a jagged rim for his vantage point. He walked to it and climbed the rim to the top.

From here he could see twenty miles. Maybe, he thought, if he saw them soon enough, he could intercept them even though he was afoot. It was the only chance he had.

He sat down on the edge of the rim. He was close to exhaustion himself. He was hungry and thirsty. He took a small drink from his canteen and held the water in his mouth for a long time before he swallowed it. He corked the canteen again even though he was thirsty still.

He thought of Abe, and he thought of his wife and of the twins. Never had he felt more alone than he did today.

He did not strain his eyes, knowing he would tire

them, and they'd betray him when he needed them. Instead, he let his glance sweep the horizon, then closer, then closer still, trying to pick out a tiny lift of dust. Once he watched a small whirlwind excitedly for five minutes before be finally decided what it was.

A wind had come up with the dawn, and had stiffened steadily, blowing out of the west. He cursed it silently. It would blow the dust of the outlaws' horses' hooves away. It might even keep him from seeing it.

Suddenly he stiffened. There it was, a sudden lift of dust that disappeared, then reappeared again. He kept his eyes on it steadily, and finally was rewarded by seeing specks at the base of the column of dust.

They were several miles away, and well to the west of him. He wasted no further time. He hurried down through the rim and off the bluff, and took an intercepting course.

He was fully aware that he was sacrificing himself. Four of them would have no trouble killing him. But he could probably get one or two before they did.

Tense and nervous, he traveled at a steady trot. When he could no longer maintain that pace, he stopped and rested until his breathing had quieted. He was bathed with sweat. His legs felt like rubber, and his head pounded. But he didn't dare rest too long. As soon as he felt able, he continued, now at a walk.

This way, he traveled for half an hour. He ought to be close to them now, he thought, and climbed the nearest knoll. At its top he stopped, again scanning the landscape, looking for that lift of dust.

Not seeing it, he scowled angrily. Where had they gone? They should now be within a quarter-mile of him. He couldn't be that far off. He had planned too carefully.

Ten minutes passed, and still he saw nothing. The velocity of the wind picked up. Now it was lifting clouds of dust and blowing them ahead of it. Panic touched Jess again. What if he had missed them? What if they had gone on by?

There was another, higher promontory south of him by a quarter-mile. Running, he headed for it, dropping blankets, saddlebags, and canteen, taking only his rifle and the revolver that hung from a holster at his side.

Panting and close to exhaustion, he reached the promontory. The air was now filled with dust. Straining his eyes, squinting, he scanned the land on all sides of him, without success.

He had missed them, and Abe would die. So would Jennie Donovan. So would her grandfather. Unless, by some miracle, he could stop the outlaws yet.

His rifle. Why hadn't he thought of it? He pointed it in the direction he thought the four must be and fired. He fired again, and again, until the gun was empty. He reloaded and waited, listening. The sound of the shots should bring them. He cast his eyes to right and left, looking for some kind of cover.

There was none. Only brush and a few rocks hardly large enough to hide his body even if he were lying prone. He selected the largest of them and crouched behind it, staring out at the windswept plain.

Dust now blew across it in blinding clouds. The sound of the wind was a high whistle. Jess saw nothing. It was as if the four outlaws had completely disappeared.

And then, at last, he understood. They were out there, all right, hidden by swirling clouds of dust. They had not heard his rifle shots, because the wind was blowing toward Jess, carrying the sound of the reports away from them.

Angrily, frantically, he emptied the gun again, reloaded, and emptied it a third time. Still he saw nothing, heard nothing.

And he was forced to the realization that he had lost. The four outlaws had gone by, and were by now well north of him. Somehow he had miscalculated their course.

He wasted no time in useless anger; in futile self-blame. Instead he returned as quickly as he could to the knoll where he had left his blankets, saddlebags, and canteen. He recovered them and once more headed north into the swirling dust.

It stung his face and choked his lungs. It filled his eyes and made him squint. He didn't bother to look for trail, but instead looked for landmarks he remembered. His legs felt like lead, and his breathing was harsh and labored.

Worst of all was the knowledge that he had failed his son. The outlaws would reach Donovan's well ahead of him. By the time he got there, it would be too late. Nothing was going to change it. No miracle was going to happen that would save Abe's life.

And it was his own savagery that was to blame. He was responsible.

Helplessly he raised a fist and shook it at the sky. Then, recognizing the futility of that, he settled down to a steady walk, one he could maintain hour after hour without exhausting himself so much that he'd have to stop. And for the first time in a long, long time, he prayed, silently and urgently, to a God he must have offended grievously with his brutality.

CHAPTER 11

THE MORE ABE THOUGHT ABOUT HIS FATHER NOT coming back, the more it worried him. At last, ten days after his father had ridden away, he knew he couldn't sit still any longer, doing nothing, just waiting for his father to return.

But he was sensible enough to know he couldn't overtake his father, even if he could find him. What he could do was what he had been preaching to his father all along. He could go to the law. He could set the law on the killers and, what with the telegraph and everything, maybe it would do some good. He knew what direction the killers were going. He knew where they had been. By using a map, it should be possible to guess what their approximate destination was and what course they would take getting there.

Having thought of it, he wondered why he hadn't thought of it before. He called to Jennie, and when she came out, he said, "I'm going in to town. Which way is it?"

She said, "You are not! You got no business trying to ride a horse!"

He said, "I'm going. Which way is town?" He got up and headed for the corral. His horse was in. Donovan had been using him for a jingle horse, to run the others in every morning. Jennie followed him, protesting. He stopped and turned. He said, "I know you mean right, and I'm beholden to you, that's sure. But I got to go. I got to try to get Pa some help. It's my fault he's alone. I figure if I can get the law in this here town to telegraph ahead, maybe somewhere down the line Pa will get some help."

"You ain't fit. You'll open up that wound."

"Maybe. But I can't sit still no more. Can't you see I can't?"

She studied his face for a long time, nodding finally. "All right. But let me saddle him."

He didn't entirely trust her not to run the horse out, so he followed her to the corral, standing in the gate opening while she caught and saddled up his horse. When the animal was ready, he asked, "Which way?"

She pointed. "There's a kind of road we made going back and forth. Just follow it."

He nodded.

Jennie asked anxiously, "You'll be back?"

He nodded. "I'll be back. If you don't mind having me."

She stood there in the yard and watched him until he went over a ridge and was lost to sight, raising a hand at the last to shield her eyes from the glare.

She wondered where Abe's father was. Dead, probably. One man cannot expect to go up against six successfully. He'd caught and killed one of them, but only because the man was wounded and had been left behind.

She tried to sort her feelings out. She wanted Abe to ask her to marry him, and she wanted to go with him, but what would her grandpa do here all alone? She couldn't leave him, even if Abe did ask.

Shaking her head impatiently, she went into the shed, got Abe's bedding, and took it into the house to wash. Abe wasn't old enough to think about taking a wife even if she was old enough to be a wife. She'd have to wait. She'd have to hope and pray that he liked her well enough to come back and see her, and maybe to come for her someday.

Busily she tackled the work in the house, wishing she could get Abe out of her mind. But a nagging thought remained. If Abe's father was dead, Abe would own the ranch where they had lived. Abe would be going back to it, and he wouldn't want to go alone.

She wasn't proud of the thought that next crossed her mind. But it stayed, and she could not make it go away.

Abe rode steadily along the two-track road Jennie had pointed out. Like Jennie, he thought it probable that his father was already dead. One man against six is not good odds, and luck cannot last indefinitely. Maybe his father had succeeded in killing another one or two of the outlaws, but if they put their mind to catching and killing him, he wouldn't have a chance.

He couldn't face the probability that his father was already dead. With his father gone, he'd be alone in the world. In a matter of a couple of weeks he'd have lost his entire family.

But supposing it *was* true? What would he do? He didn't know. He doubted his ability to run the ranch, and besides that, he knew he'd never be able to stand being all alone.

Like Jennie, he tried to drive his unwelcome thoughts away. With only indifferent success.

He reached town near noon and rode up the dusty street. It wasn't much of a town. Only a scattering of store buildings on either side of the street, and some shacks beyond, where the townspeople lived. There was a hotel, the only two-story structure in town, its clapboard sides weathered gray. There was a big corral behind the hotel, indicating that this was a stagecoach stop, where horses were changed.

Telegraph wires ran into town, and out again, the

posts diminishing in size until they disappeared over the horizon. Abe halted his horse in front of the telegraph office, which was on the ground floor of the hotel. He dismounted, and tied, and then walked down to the stone-block jail. He opened the door and went inside.

It smelled of stale tobacco smoke. A man sat at a rolltop desk, with his booted feet up on it. Abe asked, "Are you the sheriff?"

The man put his feet on the floor. He turned, and Abe saw the star on his vest. He said, "Sure am, son. Frank Bodine. What can I do for you?"

"I'm Abe Hawkins." He stopped. "Can I sit down? It's a pretty long story I've got to tell."

"Sure, boy, sit down."

Abe sat down in a straight-backed chair. He told the story of his mother's murder and the murder of his sisters as swiftly as he could. He told of his father catching up and killing one of the criminals, wondering as he did if the law would take reprisal against his father for doing so.

He finished the story and looked at the sheriff. The man's eyes were on him, half-believing, half-disbelieving. The sheriff looked down at the bandaged wound on his leg, at the place where his pants had been slit to accommodate the bandages. He said, "You say you're stayin' out at Donovan's?"

"Yes, sir. That was where my pa left me when he went on."

"And how long ago was that?"

"Week and a half, I guess."

"Them outlaws are long gone by now. So's your pa, if he's still followin'."

"Yes, sir. I figured they were."

The sheriff shuffled through a pile of papers on his

desk. He finally came up with a yellow telegram form. "Here it is. Telegram from Deer Lodge. Says seven men escaped the prison, and to be on the lookout for 'em. Leader's name was Aaron Kruse. In for murder, he was. Don't know why they didn't hang the son-of-a-bitch when they had the chance."

He stared at Abe. "What you want me to do, boy?"

"Well, sir, if you got a map, I'll show you."

The sheriff rummaged in his desk and finally brought out a dog-eared and yellowed map of the western half of the United States. He spread it out on his desk. Abe got up and stood beside him. "Where is Deer Lodge, sir?"

The sheriff pointed it out, and made an "X." Abe asked, "And where are we?"

Again the sheriff made an "X." Abe drew a line from the first "X" to the second, and on beyond. The line didn't go to Mexico. It went straight through Fort Worth. The sheriff said, "There goes your notion that they're headed for Mexico."

This realization disturbed Abe, but he couldn't argue with the map. He said, "I guess it don't matter where they're headed, sir, as long as we know where. Couldn't you telegraph Fort Worth? And maybe some of the towns in between?"

"Guess I could. Costs money, though."

Abe said, "I don't have any. When they killed my ma and the twins, they found our money and took it all."

"Well, maybe the county could pay for a couple of telegrams, even if it ain't this county's problem anymore." He studied Abe. "What you going to do now?"

Abe was angered by the sheriff's indifference. He said, "Maybe I'll go after Pa."

"That's foolishness. You'd never find him in a million years."

Abe said, "Somebody's got to do something, and you don't sound like you want to do very much."

The sheriff looked aggrieved. "Said I'd telegraph, didn't I? Even if it ain't my problem. Crimes was committed outside my county. Them escaped convicts are long gone, if they ever was in my county, which I doubt. What kind of sheriff would I be if I traipsed all over the country and let my own county go to pot?"

Abe said sullenly, "Pa said the law wouldn't do nothing. Looks to me like he was right."

"I'm doin' all I can. Now, if you don't like that, you can send them telegrams yourself."

"You know I can't."

"Then shut up about the way I do my job."

Abe got up and went outside. The sheriff followed him and walked toward the telegraph office. Abe didn't know whether he'd really send the telegrams or not, but he didn't accompany the sheriff into the telegraph office to find out.

His father had been right, sure enough, and he was the one who had been the fool. If he and his father *had* gone to the sheriff back home, they'd likely have gotten the same treatment he was getting here. Or if the sheriff had agreed to pursue the killers, he would have pursued no farther than the county line.

He wished now that he had conquered his squeamishness and let his father kill the outlaw that he'd hung from the tree by his feet. If he had, he wouldn't be here, and wounded, and his father wouldn't be pursuing the remaining killers alone, or maybe already dead.

He realized that if his father was killed, it would be a long time before he could stop blaming himself for his death.

He got his horse, mounted him, and rode out of town. He'd wasted his time coming here. A week and a half had passed, and what was going to happen had already happened.

If only he didn't feel so useless, and helpless. If only he could stop blaming himself. But what was done was done, and there was nothing he could do about it now.

But he promised himself one thing. If Kruse and his men had killed his father, he'd go after them, and find them, no matter where they went. It might take years, growing up, selling the ranch for money to travel on, learning to use a gun. But he'd do whatever it took. Only that way could he purge himself of guilt.

Jennie saw him coming and came out to stand in the yard. As he rode in, Donovan came out.

Abe dismounted, wincing as his wounded leg took his weight. He said, "My pa was right. He wouldn't do anything."

"Wouldn't he even send the telegrams?"

"He said he would, but I think he lied. He was bellyaching about what it cost to send a couple of telegrams."

Jennie said, "Let me put away your horse."

He let her take the reins. He sank down onto a bench beside the door. Donovan said, "I heard."

Abe asked, "What do you think I ought to do?"

"What your pa told you to do. You go traipsin' off now, an' he'll just have to come after you. Besides, you ain't healed up yet. Supposin' that wound starts festerin'?"

Abe nodded reluctantly. Donovan was right. He'd done what he could, and now all he could do was wait.

CHAPTER 12

AARON KRUSE WAS BIGGER AND HEAVIER THAN JESS. Though he was tall, his legs were short, and bowed, and looked hardly strong enough to support the weight of his powerful upper body.

His hair, which had been kept shaved at Deer Lodge, was now growing out. It made a graying stubble on his head. He hadn't shaved since leaving the prison, and now half an inch of stubble covered his dirty face.

His eyes seemed almost lost in the folds of flesh surrounding them, but once you had seen them, you weren't likely to forget what they were like. Close-set and small, when they rested on you they put a chill in you. As gray as bullets, they were more like the eyes of a predatory animal than those of a man. It was as if everything they looked upon was viewed as prey to be killed, if not for a reason, then for the sheer sport of it.

Kruse liked baiting other men, and when they fought back, killed them with his great hands and powerful arms. He could embrace a man and break his ribs. He could make him scream with pain before he dropped him, unconscious and sometimes dead. The warden at Deer Lodge had considered Kruse his most dangerous prisoner. The warden wasn't given to fearing his prisoners, but he had been afraid of Kruse.

Kruse ruled the six men with him as unyieldingly outside the prison as he had ruled them inside its walls. He himself had raped Edie Hawkins first, and then had watched, grinning, as his men took turns. When the twins screamed and screamed and would not stop, Kruse had killed them by knocking their heads against the wall of the house.

He had left Lawson behind, when he was wounded, as unfeelingly as he had murdered the Hawkins twins, and if he'd known Vigil was going back to help Lawson, he'd have stopped him. But he hadn't known. And Vigil had later returned to camp babbling in terror about what had been done to Lawson before he died.

Kruse hadn't counted on the woman's husband following. The damn fool must know seven men had been involved in the attack on his family. He ought to have sense enough not to try going up against seven such as these. Even if he did have his son along with him.

Not long afterward, the man pursuing them caught Claggett gathering firewood. He strung him up by the ankles and would have cut him like a calf if the son hadn't interfered. Claggett escaped, after wounding the boy. And Kruse had thought they'd finally seen the last of the avenging husband and his son.

Not so. Several nights later, Claggett awakened them with his goddamned gurgling. His throat had been cut, and he was choking to death on his own blood. The trail Kruse found said the man was now alone. He'd left his wounded son someplace and had come on by himself.

They followed, of course, as soon as it was light. But not long afterward, Kruse ordered them to halt. He said, "For Christ's sake, this is what he wants. If we're chasing him, he can lay an ambush for us anytime."

"What else can we do?" Vigil asked.

"By God, we can head back to where he left his kid and force his hand. He'll get careless if he knows we're going after his kid. And once we get our hands on the boy, we can make him give himself up. Then we can kill 'em both and get them off our backs."

Helfer said, "That way will cost us more'n a week. I

say let's go on. If we're careful, he ain't goin' to get no more of us."

Kruse put those tiny, bullet-gray eyes on him. "Who asked you to open your big mouth?"

Helfer tried to meet his glance. He couldn't, and looked away. Kruse said, "Come on. We're going back."

Already there was a balked and smoldering fury in Aaron Kruse. They were supposed to meet Domingo Chavez, who had been released from Deer Lodge six months earlier, in Fort Worth by October 1. Chavez had wanted Kruse and six men for an army payroll robbery. Now Kruse was down to four, and if he lost any more, they'd be too short-handed to pull off the robbery. Well, Chavez would have to get another man or two in Fort Worth. If he couldn't, they'd just make do with what they had. But it was damned important that he didn't lose any more. Chavez wanted men like these, who had nothing to lose. There would be an escort with the paymaster's wagon. They all had to die, so that the army would think it had been an Indian attack. Nowadays, Indians knew what money was. They knew it would buy guns, and they took it whenever they could get their hands on it. So the fact that the money was taken wouldn't automatically rule out Indians.

Kruse suspected that the bluff might be a logical spot for Hawkins to ambush them. He put out flankers to guard against an ambush, and waved them on to the top of the bluff, believing that would force the ambusher to flee. It caught him completely by surprise when Hawkins commenced firing from the rocks at the foot of the bluff. Hell, there was no place there to hide a horse, and he'd figured no one would be fool enough to ambush five men on horseback when he himself was afoot.

Vigil went down, and the rest of them scattered, with Kruse bellowing angrily that now they had the son-of-a-bitch. But they hadn't. Hawkins had thrown his horse. He let him up, and mounted, and got clean away.

Kruse was livid with rage. But he still didn't waste time trying to track Hawkins down. He kept on heading north along Hawkins' back trail, knowing Hawkins would have to come to him. Next time, he wouldn't get caught unaware. Next time, he'd anticipate the ambush and catch Hawkins. When he did, he'd make the man beg for death before he was through with him.

They went on. Kruse ordered them to build no fires when they camped. He circled every possible ambush site. A wind came up, and nearly blew away the trail. But they picked it up again farther on, and continued toward wherever it was that Hawkins had left his son. They didn't see the man again.

Near sundown, the wind diminished and the dust clouds began to settle. Jess Hawkins began again to look for trail. The trail of four horsemen should not be difficult to find, particularly since they were leading two extra horses.

He found it just as the sky was getting dark, confirming what he had guessed before, that the outlaws had passed him during the windstorm and were now ahead of him.

There was no longer much chance that he could reach Donovan's in time to save Abe's life and the lives of Jennie Donovan and her grandfather. But if there was a chance, it lay in obtaining a fresh horse.

How to do that out here, Jess had no idea. He was dead-tired. He was hungry and thirsty, and his feet ached abominably. To make it worse, the leather of his boots was wearing out. Already the seam at one side of his right boot had split open, and there was a hole in the sole. He cut pieces of leather from his pistol holster and fitted them inside both boots, afterward shoving the revolver down into his belt. He drank a little water. Then he lay down to sleep.

Nightmares haunted his sleep. He awoke an hour before dawn, and as soon as it was light enough to see the trail, began walking once again. He was ravenous by now, and growing weak, but in midmorning he spotted something that made him break into a run. It was the carcass of one of the convicts' horses that had gone lame and had been shot.

With trembling hands he hacked chunks of meat from the horse's hindquarters. He laid them on a rock, and as quickly as he could, gathered buffalo chips and got a fire started. He ate the first chunk of meat half-raw. By the time the last had cooked, his stomach was full.

His feet still hurt, but he could feel his strength returning. He cut off several more chunks, enough to last him several days, and stuffed the bloody meat into one of his saddlebags. He went on, hurrying now to make up lost time.

No longer did he try slavishly to follow trail. Instead, he ranged to the right and left of it, staying on high ground, looking for horses, for cattle, for smoke, or for other signs of habitation.

He traveled most of the day without seeing anything. Then, near sundown, he spotted a tiny pillar of dust a couple of miles away.

Reaching the highest point of ground available, he squatted and studied it. Eventually he made out two horsemen at the foot of it. They were heading for a stream bed in which some scrub willows and stunted cottonwoods grew.

Jess walked toward the place, careful to stay in whatever low ground he could find so that he would not be seen. He felt a fierce exultation at the prospect of getting a horse to ride, and he was a little surprised at himself when he realized that he was going to take it, by force if necessary. He examined his own thoughts and admitted that, if there was no other way, he would kill for it.

This, then, was what the escaped convicts had done to him. They had changed him from a peaceful man who asked nothing of anyone into a predator like themselves, prepared to kill for what he needed.

Yet, even though he despised what he might have to do, he did not hesitate. Abe's life was at stake. So were Jennie's and Donovan's. So were other lives, of innocents who happened to be in the path the outlaws would take when they left Donovan's.

The sun went down. The clouds flamed and then faded, and the sky deepened its color until it was almost dark.

A fire winked ahead, sometimes hidden by brush and trees, sometimes visible. From a quarter mile, Hawkins crept in like a stalking cat. Three hundred yards away he became even more catlike, testing each footstep before he put his weight down, moving on a cautious step at a time.

There were two men at the fire. Both were Indians. They had apparently been hunting, because they had two deer hanging in a nearby tree.

Jess realized that he would have to take both their horses. He didn't dare take only one, because if he did, they would certainly pursue.

Standing there in the darkness fifty yards beyond the

perimeter of their fire's light, Jess knew he ought to kill them both, instantly and without hesitation. It was the only way of being sure. He put down everything he was carrying.

He raised his rifle and sighted it carefully. His finger tightened on the trigger.

And then it froze. Try as he would, he could not fire. With a soft grunt of disgust at himself, he lowered the gun.

Carefully, the stalking cat once more, he went on. At last he could step into the firelight, unseen and unheard, and he did.

One Indian was squatting at the fire, turning some meat cooking on a spit. The other was getting ready to hobble the horses. Jess said softly, "Don't move, either one of you!"

Neither Indian had a gun within his reach. Both looked at him, tensed as if to run; then they relaxed as they realized the futility of trying to get away. Jess said, "I just want your horses, boys."

With the rifle ready, he crossed the little clearing. He waved the Indian beside the horses away from them. The man backed, half-crouched, and Jess knew he wasn't going to be allowed to mount unmolested. The instant he was distracted, even slightly, both Indians would move. They'd either run at him with their knives, or they'd go for their guns.

He moved fast for so big a man. Like a charging bear, he rushed the Indian who had been with the horses. Clubbing his rifle, he struck the brave on the side of the head. The man went down, and didn't move.

But the other one had moved. He was coming, knife gleaming in his hand. Whirling, in a half-crouch, Jess fired instantly. The bullet struck, but it couldn't stop the

Indian's momentum. Jess jumped aside, and the Indian charged on past, to fall ten feet beyond.

Damn! He hadn't wanted to hurt either one of them. But there was no use regretting something that could not be changed. Jess was fighting for Abe's life, and his own.

The horses had spooked away from the gunshot. Speaking soothingly, Jess pursued them, and finally caught them both. He tied the reins of one to the other's tail, then mounted that one and rode out. He picked up his blanket roll and saddlebags where he had left them.

Behind him, as he mounted once again, he heard the Indians talking in guttural excited tones. Neither, then, was dead. The realization made him feel better, but not very much.

In his own eyes, he had become a criminal. He had taken, by violence, something that did not belong to him. He had left the Indians afoot, and hurt, and he knew they both might die.

Maybe Abe had been right. Maybe he should have gone to the law. Because even now there was no assurance that he would arrive at Donovan's in time to prevent the convicts from killing Abe and Jennie and Donovan.

CHAPTER 13

SHERIFF FRANK BODINE SENT THE FIRST TELEGRAM TO Fort Worth. He said he had information that Kruse and his companions were on their way to Fort Worth. He requested that he be advised.

Then he waited. Two hours later, he got a reply. Kruse had not been seen, but a careful watch for him would be kept.

Bodine left the telegraph office, well-satisfied with himself. If Kruse showed up in Fort Worth, and was captured or killed, he would, by sending one telegram, have established a claim to part of the reward. Five hundred dollars each, for six men, added up to three thousand dollars. Even if he got only a fourth, it would be a substantial sum.

He went back to his office. He began to think that if he knew the location of the man Jess Hawkins had staked out and killed, he could get the body and collect a five-hundred-dollar reward all for himself.

That was damn near a whole year's pay. It was worth working on. He would ride out to Donovan's first thing in the morning and find out what he could from Abe. Maybe the kid couldn't tell him exactly where the body was. But he might be able to tell him enough so that he could find it in a day or two. It would be decomposed, and it would stink like hell, but it would still be recognizable. He could have a photograph taken as soon as he got the body back to town. That would be enough to establish his claim to the reward.

He slept very little that night, thinking all the time of the reward. Five hundred would buy him a piece of land to retire on. With what he had, he could build a house and buy a few cattle. He wouldn't have to worry any more about getting old and being unable to work.

It never occurred to him that Hawkins was entitled to the reward. But if he had thought of it, he would have rationalized that Hawkins had gone off and left the body to rot, thereby giving up any claim that he might have had.

He was up early, and by sunup was on his way out to Donovan's. He reached it in midmorning, but halted instantly as he crested the last rise and looked down at it. There were five saddled horses tied in the yard. There was one in the corral.

The horses might, of course, belong to members of a posse trailing the escaped convicts. But they might also belong to the convicts themselves. Why they would return and end up at Donovan's, he had no idea, of course, but it was a possibility.

He backed off and tied his horse to a clump of brush, out of sight of the house. He crawled back to the crest of the rise and lay on his stomach, staring down. After a time, Jennie Donovan came out, accompanied by a man. She went to the outhouse, and the man waited outside. After several minutes she came out and returned to the house. The man followed her, apparently making remarks she didn't like, because she broke into a run.

That much told Sheriff Bodine what he wanted to know. The horses down in Donovan's yard belonged to Kruse and his outlaw friends. Incredible as it seemed, it was true.

Five horses. Jess Hawkins must have killed another of them. Bodine couldn't know that one of the five horses was the buggy horse stolen from Hawkins' corral. He couldn't know there were only four outlaws at Donovan's instead of five.

He'd hoped to discover the whereabouts of the dead outlaw and thus collect five hundred dollars reward money for himself. Now he was looking at four or five times that. But he was also facing greater danger and difficulty. The outlaws were vicious and desperate. There wasn't a chance that one man could capture them.

He would need a posse. Swiftly he backed off the knoll. He got up, untied his horse, mounted, and rode back toward town. Not until he was a quarter-mile away did he spur the horse into a lope.

He reached town a little after noon. He went immediately to the hotel, in front of which there was a bell. It was rung for fires and celebrations, and he rang it now, loudly and urgently.

People poured out of their doors and came hurrying toward the hotel. Bodine waited until all had gathered. Then he raised his hands. “I need about ten men. Them outlaws that escaped from Deer Lodge are out at Donovan’s.”

He waited until the babble of voices died down, and then he yelled, “Each of you gets ten dollars for every one of ’em that we capture or kill. I figure there’s five of ’em out there. That’s fifty apiece for you.”

Someone yelled, “I’ll go! Hell, that’s damn near two months’ pay!”

Others yelled their willingness. Bodine called the names of ten of them and told them to get their horses and guns, if they had any. If not, he said he’d issue rifles from the rack in the sheriff’s office.

It took them twenty minutes to get their horses and gather in front of the jail. During that time, Bodine got himself a fresh mount at the livery barn. He handed out rifles and ammunition to those who didn’t have them. He had the ten men raise their right hands, and swore them in. Then he mounted and led them out of town.

He held his horse to a trot most of the way, because he didn’t want them to arrive with their horses all worn out. The outlaws might conceivably have left Donovan’s, and if they had, he wanted the horses in shape to take up the pursuit.

They reached Donovan’s in late afternoon. The sun was low in the western sky, but it wouldn’t set for an hour yet. They stopped behind the knoll where the sheriff had lain earlier today. The town blacksmith,

Smathers, asked, "What about Donovan an' his girl? We can't just start shootin' into the house."

Bodine said, "We'll give them convicts a chance to give up. If they don't, well, I reckon Donovan an' his girl will just have to take their chances."

The blacksmith opened his mouth to protest again, then closed it without saying anything. He looked away from Bodine as if he was ashamed, and the sheriff knew he was thinking about the fifty dollars he would get when the outlaws were dead or in custody. He was thinking about getting the fifty, but he didn't want to expose himself to the convicts' fire earning it.

Bodine said, "All right, then. Smathers, you take Jones and Rodrigues and circle around to the other side." He sent three men to take positions on the northern side of Donovan's, and two to take positions on the south. He kept two with him. He watched from the knoll, mostly hidden, until they were in place.

Then he raised up and yelled, "Hey, down at the house! You're surrounded! Give yourselves up, and nobody will get hurt!"

If he'd had any doubts about the men at Donovan's being the wanted convicts, they were dispelled by the almost instantaneous gunfire that crackled from the windows and door of the house. He raised an arm and yelled to his own men an unnecessary command, "Commence firing!" Already they were pouring bullets toward the shack.

Bodine let them fire for a couple of minutes until their guns were emptied. Then, in the silence that came while they reloaded, he yelled, "Cease firing!"

They all looked at him. To the men down below he bawled, "Ready to give up now?"

A man came to the door. He stepped outside, a bull of

a man whose upper half seemed too heavy for his spindly legs. His roaring voice carried easily to the knoll. "No, but I got some word for you. Git your asses back to town, or we'll kill the old man down here and throw his carcass out."

Bodine had been willing to shoot into the cabin and let Donovan and his girl take their chances with the others, chances that were pretty good, since they'd have taken cover and the outlaws would be partially exposed. But he didn't see how he could continue on a course that would result in Donovan's certain death. While he hesitated, the man down below bellowed, "An' if that ain't enough, we'll strip this pretty little filly an' use her an' then throw her out with the old man! But if that don't do it, we'll throw this kid out with them."

Bodine stood up. "All right!"

The man down below roared, "Gut on back to town. I'll send a man out pretty soon to make sure you're gone. If he don't come back, well, that's the end of the old man, the kid, an' the girl!"

Bodine waved his men toward him. The man in the doorway down below disappeared. When all the men were in, Bodine said, "Come on. We're going part way to town, at least. Far enough so's he'll think we're gone."

"And then what?"

Irritably Bodine snapped, "How the hell do I know? But I can't stay here and watch while he kills those three people."

A man said, "He'll kill 'em anyway when he leaves. Or he'll take 'em along for hostages."

"If he does, then we'll have to figure out something else." He led the way, and the men followed him, grumbling sourly. They didn't want to lose the fifty dollars that had been promised them. Few of them knew Donovan very well anyway.

Bodine led them away a mile, then down into a long gully where they'd be hidden from the man the outlaw had said he'd send out to check. Bodine himself eased back to the top of the ridge and lay down to watch.

Sure enough, a man rode to the top of the knoll and stared toward him. Apparently satisfied, the man rode back and disappeared.

Bodine returned to his men in the gully. "Stay here," he said. "If I want you, I'll fire three quick shots."

One asked, "What are you fixin' to do?"

"Watch. Maybe something will happen to change the way things are now." He didn't see what could happen. But he did know the outlaws couldn't stay forever at Donovan's. They thought they had made him return to town, and they'd figure he had wired for more help.

Why were they at Donovan's, anyway? It didn't seem to make any sense. They'd been a long way south, and they'd come back. There had to be a reason, but at the moment Bodine couldn't figure out what it could be.

He reached the knoll and tied his horse to a clump of brush, out of sight below its crest. He started to ease to the top of the knoll to look.

Behind him he heard the hoof-beats of a trotting horse. Turning his head, he saw a man riding toward him.

The man was riding a pinto horse, without a saddle, with an Indian bridle on him. He halted in front of Bodine, looked at the star on his vest, and said, "I'm Jess Hawkins. Are those convicts down there at Donovan's?"

The man was gaunt and hollow-eyed. There was a half-inch growth of whiskers on his haggard face. He was covered with dust, and he looked beat. Bodine nodded.

"Is my boy all right?"

"So far."

A look of relief so great it completely changed the man came over Hawkins' face. "And Donovan and the girl?"

"All right, so far. That big one made us pull back and head for town. Said he'd kill 'em all if we didn't."

Hawkins slid off his horse. He tied him near the sheriff's, then followed him to the top of the knoll, crawling the last few yards. Bodine asked, "What now?"

Hawkins said, "They're after me. They came back here knowin' I'd follow them. If they was to know I was here, they'd likely come after me."

Bodine shook his head. "Why should they? They've got your son. All they've got to do is threaten to kill him, and you'll come to them."

Hawkins shook his head. "No, I won't. No matter what they do. Because I know that if they got me, they'd kill me, and them three down there too."

"You want me to get out of sight?"

Hawkins nodded. "You keep a lookout. When they come after me, I'll hold 'em as long as I can. Then I'll pull back and give you a chance to get between them and the shack."

Bodine stared doubtfully at him. But finally he nodded agreement. He eased back down the hill, got his horse, and rode away, occasionally looking back at Jess Hawkins lying prone on top of the knoll.

He didn't like this arrangement, but he had to admit it was better than anything he'd been able to come up with.

CHAPTER 14

AS SOON AS HELFER RETURNED FROM MAKING SURE the sheriff and his posse had withdrawn, Kruse asked, "How many horses in that corral out there?"

"One."

Kruse said, "Go on out and saddle him."

"We leavin'?"

"Yeah, we're leavin'. It don't look like that damn Hawkins is ever goin' to get here. Maybe one of us hit him and he's layin' back there dead. Or maybe his horse died and left him afoot. If we run into him, we'll kill the son-of-a-bitch, but we ain't goin' to hang around here no more."

"What about the sheriff? He sure as hell didn't go all the way back to town. There's likely about two, three hundred apiece on us, and he ain't goin' to give *that* up."

"I know that. That's why we're takin' these three along with us."

Helfer headed toward the door. Kruse said, "Go out with him, Juan, and keep a lookout."

Juan García went out with Helfer. The door closed again. Kruse looked at Jennie. "Put all the food you got into a gunnysack. You better not leave anything, because me and my friends are goin' to eat whether you three do or not."

Jennie, white-faced and scared, got a gunnysack. Abe got up from where he sat at the rear of the cabin and limped after her, holding the sack while she put in the food. Kruse said, "Gore, get all the canteens off the saddles an' fill 'em up."

Gore went out the door, a scowling man who since

coming here had watched Jennie's every move, the way a cat watches a mouse that is just out of its reach. The sound of the pump squeaking came in through the half-open door.

To Abe, Jennie whispered, "Abe, I'm scared." She was shaking all over, and there wasn't anything reassuring he could say to her. They were going to be used as hostages to guarantee the outlaws' safety from the sheriff and his posse. Kruse knew as well as Abe did that the sheriff had withdrawn only far enough to keep from being seen. He hadn't given up.

Abe had a sudden premonition that all three of them were going to die. Kruse and the others would use them as hostages now, but when and if they got clear, they sure wouldn't release any one of them. He remembered the way his mother and twin sisters had looked lying dead back home in the yard. He remembered the old man and his wife. He wanted to do something, but he was smart enough to know that resistance now would only hasten the end. If they went along without resistance, there was always a chance that something would happen to change what now looked impossible.

He supposed Kruse was right. His father *was* dead. If he wasn't here by now, it was almost sure. He wished that he hadn't interfered in what his father had tried to do to the outlaw that he'd caught. Things might have been different if he had not. At least one more of the outlaws would probably have been dead. His father might still be alive.

He made up his mind, quietly, that one way or another he would finish what his father had begun. Maybe he didn't have the stomach to do what his father had done or tried to do to the men he'd caught. But he *could* kill them. Knowing that his own, Donovan's, and

Jennie's lives were at stake, he could kill. All he needed was the chance.

Gore came back in, having filled the canteens and hung them from their respective saddles. He eyed Jennie, and Abe deliberately stepped in front of her. Gore looked at him with his cold gray eyes in a way that made a ball of ice form in Abe's chest. Juan García, the slight one, came in and said, "We're ready when you are."

Kruse looked at Donovan. "You first, old man. Don't try gettin' away, or this girl will . . . well, you know what I'm talkin' about."

Gore said, "There's only six horses, and there's seven of us. The gal's goin' to have to ride double with somebody."

Kruse stared at him. "And you want her to ride with you. That it?"

"Why not?"

Abe could feel Jennie trembling violently behind him. He knew he ought to object and to fight if necessary, but he also knew that to fight now would be stupid, because there wasn't too much Gore could do to Jennie on a horse. Juan García was grinning. "How about letting her ride with me? Gore'll have her black and blue all over from pinchin' her."

Kruse said, "Shut up, both of you. I ain't goin' to have the bunch of you fightin' over that damn girl. She'll ride with the kid."

Abe heard his own breath sigh slowly out, and realized he had been holding it. Jennie was still trembling as she followed him out the door. He boosted her up onto his horse, tied on the gunnysack, and mounted behind her. Donovan got on the buggy horse that the outlaws had stolen back at the Hawkins ranch.

There was no saddle on the horse, but Donovan didn't seem to mind. The outlaws mounted, one by one, and Kruse led out. Donovan followed, and Abe and Jennie followed Donovan. The other three outlaws—Gore, García, and Helfer—brought up the rear.

Abe stared around at the horizon carefully. Once he thought he saw something move up on a ridge directly in front of the house, but he kept watching, and did not see it again. He decided he had imagined it.

Behind him, Helfer said, "Maybe the damn sheriff *did* go back to town."

Kruse said, "Huh-uh. He's over there someplace watchin' us. He'll be along."

Jennie, in front of Abe, was still trembling. She was warm, and soft, and she stirred him with her nearness in a way he had never been stirred before. He felt ashamed, feeling this way when Jennie was so scared, but he couldn't help himself.

They maintained a steady trot, heading south. Abe kept looking back, but it was a long, long time before he saw anybody following. Then he saw a lifting cloud of dust and some horsemen at its base, made tiny by distance but plainly visible.

Kruse, who had also been looking back, said, "There they are."

All of the outlaws looked around. Except for Gore. He kept his eyes on Jennie. Abe thought of what Gore, and the others, had done to his mother before she died. Gore had the same thing in mind for Jennie. The thought made Abe hot with fury. It made his knees begin to shake. He was afraid of Gore, but he knew that sooner or later he was probably going to have to fight the man. And when he did, it would have to be with guns, because guns were the only thing that would equalize the two.

Helfer called, "What do you reckon that sheriff's goin' to do?"

Kruse shrugged noncommittally. "He'll follow us awhile. He'll likely give up in a hundred miles or so."

"What if he don't?"

"Then he'll likely try jumping us."

"Even while we got them hostages?"

"All that damn lawman can see right now is dollar signs. He pulled back once, but that was when he knew right where we was. He ain't likely to hold off a second time."

"Then why the hell did we bother to bring hostages?"

Kruse grinned. "Well, now, I like the girl. And if we should run into Hawkins on the way south, it ain't goin' to hurt to have his kid."

There was no more talk after that. At a steady trot, they continued south, slowing to a walk only to climb some steep slope or to descend into a ravine.

Noon came, but they did not stop. At the crest of each ridge, Kruse looked behind. So did Abe, and it soon became obvious that the sheriff and his posse were gaining gradually on them.

From its zenith, the sun began to drop in the western sky. Abe thought about the coming night. He knew the outlaws weren't going to let Jennie alone. He knew that he and Jennie's grandfather would have to watch what happened, probably tied so they couldn't intervene.

Abe, whose feelings since the murder of his mother and twin sisters had been tortured and confused, who had been torn between a thirst to avenge them and revulsion at the things his father did or tried to do to their killers, now was beginning to think more like his father did. These weren't men—not in the sense that one usually thinks of men. They had no mercy, no decency, no pity for their victims. They did not deserve easy deaths.

Looking back, he could see that the sheriff and his posse were now less than three-quarters of a mile behind. And he conceived a desperate plan. Jennie wouldn't like it, but he knew her grandfather would approve.

He jogged along with his head down, as though dozing. Three of the outlaws were behind him, one ahead. The terrain had to be exactly right, or he would fail.

CHAPTER 15

LYING ON THE CREST OF THE KNOLL, JESS HAWKINS saw Helfer come out of the cabin, followed by Juan García, the skinny one. He saw Helfer go to the corral, catch Abe's horse, head him out and saddle him, while Juan scanned the surrounding slopes watchfully. He understood, even before another of the men came out and began refilling canteens, that the four outlaws were leaving Donovan's. The presence of the sheriff and his posse had scared them off. They probably thought that he was dead or that his horse had given out and left him afoot. In any case, they figured they no longer had to be afraid of him.

Saddling Abe's horse might only mean they were stealing him. But he couldn't believe that, however much he wanted to. What it probably meant was that they were simply taking Donovan, Jennie, and Abe along as hostages.

Hawkins had no doubt about what would happen to the three hostages when the outlaws finally got away.

They wouldn't be released. They'd be slaughtered without pity just as had Jess's own family, just as had the old man and woman whose ranch house the outlaws had invaded on their way south.

But Hawkins did know one thing. Alone, he'd have no chance of getting the hostages safely away. He might kill one or two of the outlaws, but those remaining would retaliate by killing or torturing the hostages. No. In this he needed the sheriff's help.

He watched the outlaws come out of the cabin and mount. He watched Donovan jump onto the buggy horse the outlaws had stolen out of Jess's own corral. He watched Abe boost Jennie onto his horse, tie on a sack that probably contained provisions, and then mount behind her. The whole cavalcade trotted out of Donovan's yard, heading south.

Jess waited until they had gone over a ridge and were lost to sight. Then he got up. He walked to where his horse stood munching grass, mounted, and rode toward where he knew the sheriff and his posse were.

He encountered the sheriff first. He said, "They've gone."

"And you let 'em? You didn't try to stop them?"

Jess said, "They took Donovan, Jennie, and my son as hostages."

"Well, let's get after them." The sheriff hurried back toward the place he had left his horse.

Jess kept pace. He asked, "What do you plan to do?"

"Well, by God, I don't plan to let 'em get away."

"What about the hostages?"

"They won't hurt 'em. They know they'd have to answer for it if they did."

By now the sheriff had reached his horse. He mounted. Jess said angrily, "What the hell are you talking about? Those four can kill all they damn please, and they still won't have any more to answer for than they already do. They've killed before. Why should they hesitate to kill again if they think it might save their hides?"

The sheriff said stiffly, "I got my duty to do."

Jess Hawkins raged, "Duty? You son-of-a-bitch, all you're thinking about is the five hundred dollars that's on the head of each of them outlaws. If there wasn't no reward, you'd be back in your office sitting on your big fat butt!"

The sheriff's face flushed. "Watch your tongue, Hawkins! I don't have to take that kind of abuse from you!"

Jess Hawkins clenched his fists. Fighting with the sheriff wasn't going to accomplish anything. He hadn't brought the sheriff and his posse here, and even if he had gone on without them, they'd have caught up eventually. He'd just have to hope he could hold them back and keep them from endangering the hostages. He wasn't proud of himself for thinking with reluctant relief that Donovan would be the first that the outlaws killed. But Abe would be second. They would save Jennie until the last.

Only be didn't want anybody to be killed. And that meant letting the outlaws alone, for the time being, at least. They could follow along behind, but the minute they threatened the four, Donovan would be in deadly jeopardy.

They came in sight of the place where the posse was waiting, and the sheriff shouted for them to saddle up. The men saddled quickly, mounted, and gathered around the sheriff and Jess.

Bodine said, "Them four have headed south."

One of the ten posse said, "I thought you said there was five."

"Hawkins says there's only four. I guess they had an extra horse." He waited an instant and then went on, "They've taken Donovan, his girl, and this man's son as hostages. I figure they'll kill 'em if we get too close. So we'll just follow along for now and see what turns up."

Another of the men said, "For how long? Hell, I say let's surround 'em and take 'em right away. They ain't going to hurt Donovan or his girl or this man's kid when they know they ain't got no chance."

Several others chorused agreement. One man said, "I can't go traipsin' all over the countryside when it ain't even needful."

Bodine looked at Hawkins, then back at his posse. "You'll do what I say, or you can go back to town. Is that understood?"

The men grumbled sullenly. Bodine said, "I mean it. Any of you that don't feel like being gone a week or so had just as well go back home now."

More grumbling. A couple of the men left and headed back toward town. The other eight remained. Bodine said sourly, "All right, then, let's go."

The sheriff rode at the head of his men, scowling. In ten minutes they picked up the trail, but when they finally caught sight of the fleeing outlaws ahead, the outlaws had a lead of a mile and a half. The sheriff's scowl gradually faded and went away, but the smoldering anger remained in his eyes.

He was squarely between Hawkins and his posse, and he hadn't yet taken a firm position for himself. Being sheriff, he knew Donovan and Jennie too. He didn't want to see them killed. On the other hand, he didn't see how they could be safely rescued, and he didn't want to risk losing the rewards.

They had been riding for about ten miles when he turned his head and spoke to Jess. "What about you?"

"What do you mean?"

"What about the rewards? You figure on claimin' part of them?"

Jess said disgustedly, "Oh, for Christ's sake! Is that all you been thinking about?"

The sheriff's eyes glittered. He said, "I asked you a question."

Jess said, "Hell no, I don't want no damn rewards. I don't even care if I get back the money they stole from me. All I want is to see their carcasses stretched out rotting in the sun."

The sheriff said stiffly, "There will be no executions when we catch up with them. We're going to do it lawfully."

Jess Hawkins grunted sourly. There was no use arguing that point, but if it was up to him, the law was through with the outlaw crew. They'd had their chance, and had sent the men to Deer Lodge, but they hadn't been able to keep them there. Because they hadn't, at least five people were dead, and more would be before all this was through.

For a time they rode in silence. Finally Hawkins said, "If it comes to parleying with them, don't let them know that I'm along. They likely think I'm dead, but they want me almost as bad as I want them. They're liable to do anything to the hostages to make me give myself up to them."

Bodine nodded. "All right. But I doubt if we'll be doing any parleying."

The sun climbed slowly to its zenith, then started down toward the horizon in the west. The distance between posse and outlaw gang had narrowed to about three-quarters of a mile. Hawkins could make out the outlaw leader riding at their head. Abe and Jennie, riding double, followed him. Donovan, riding bareback on the buggy horse, came third. The other outlaws brought up the rear.

It was maddening to Jess to see the men he wanted so very close to him. But there wasn't anything he could do but wait.

Abe kept watch all during the early afternoon for just the right kind of terrain in which to attempt escape. He would have to ride past Helfer, Gore, and García.

What he was counting on was taking them by surprise. He doubted if attempting escape would put any of them in any greater danger than what they already were in. Jennie was almost certain to be molested by the outlaws when darkness came. He or Donovan, or both of them, might well be killed if they tried to intervene. Besides, he told himself, when he made his escape attempt, his body would be between Jennie and the outlaws' guns. He'd catch their bullets before she did.

Kruse was climbing a steep slope now, at the top of which there was a ten-foot rim. When he reached the top, he had to turn and follow the rim for about a hundred yards to reach a fissure that would permit his horse to climb out through the rim to the top of the little butte. Abe waited until all six horses had reached the rim and had turned to parallel it. Then he reined hard right and dug his heels into his horse's sides.

The horse knew him, and he knew the horse. Instantly the animal plunged down the steep slope, sliding sometimes, once nearly losing his footing and tumbling end-over-end. Abe could see the ten men of the sheriff's posse approaching less than half a mile away. If he could reach them before he was shot down or overtaken . . .

The sack of grub banged against the horse's flanks with every lunge. It frightened him, and he plunged downward even more swiftly than before.

Jennie screamed with fear. Behind them, guns racketed, and bullets ricocheted from rocks they struck on the slope.

Abe's back ached in expectation of a bullet striking it. Jennie screamed again. She tried to seize the reins from Abe. She wailed, "Grandpa! We can't leave Grandpa!"

That had been the thing that had worried Abe. He had settled it with himself, because be had known that their staying wouldn't improve Donovan's chances one bit. If anything, Donovan would be safer if they got away, because he would be the only hostage they had left.

Fighting Jennie for the reins, Abe looked up desperately toward the posse. He was relieved to see that they were approaching at a gallop.

But his relief was short-lived. Jennie managed to get the reins briefly away from him. In her terror she didn't use her head. She pulled the horse's head around, trying to turn him back.

The horse, with his head pulled around, missed his footing on the slope. He went down, forequarters first, throwing both Jennie and Abe on ahead of him.

Fortunately for them both, he was close to the bottom of the slope. They struck a little beyond its foot, not in the jumble of sharp-pointed rocks broken off the rim by the ages, but beyond, in high grass and on smooth ground.

Abe was partly stunned, but not stunned enough to forget that the horse was tumbling down the slope immediately behind. He let himself roll, and felt Jennie as he collided violently with her. He heard the horse's shrill neigh of terror, and from the corner of one eye glimpsed the huge body somersaulting toward him.

He grabbed Jennie's arm and lunged away, dragging her along with him. The horse struck on his back where Jennie had lain only a moment before.

Jennie was as stunned as Abe. Both were covered with dust, choking in a cloud of it. The horse lay still for a moment before scrambling to his feet, apparently unhurt.

Abe heard rifle shots, all of them very close. He heard the hooves of horses, and the cascading rocks they dislodged on the slope. He struggled to his feet, and then pulled Jennie up. She favored one leg, which apparently she had hurt.

Abe started to dust himself off, but he never got a chance to finish. Something hit him in the mouth, and he felt his lips smashed and crushed and split against his teeth.

He hit the ground on his back. Before he had more than realized what had happened to him, he was yanked to his feet. Once more Kruse's fist smashed his mouth, turned numb by that first vicious blow.

Again and again Kruse struck, holding Abe erect with his left band while he struck him with the right.

Abe's senses faded. The sky and the clouds and the hard faces of the outlaws whirled before his eyes. He heard Jennie sobbing hysterically. And then everything went black.

CHAPTER 16

JESS HAWKINS SAW HIS SON, WITH JENNIE RIDING ahead, break away from the others and come plunging recklessly down the steep, rocky slope. Dust rose in clouds behind his horse, obscuring the pursuing outlaws and Donovan. He roared, "Come on!" and dug spurs into his horse's sides so savagely that the animal literally jumped into the air and hit the ground running. Jess was half a dozen yards ahead of Bodine and his posse before they too saw the opportunity and spurred their horses into a ran.

Only a quarter-mile now separated them from the outlaws plunging down the slope. Jess prayed silently that they would not simply kill both Abe and Jennie to prevent their escape.

He jacked a cartridge into his rifle, which, for lack of a scabbard, he carried across his knees.

Then, just as Abe's sliding, plunging, terrified horse was almost to the bottom, he fell, somersaulting, throwing both Abe and Jennie ahead of him.

Jess literally held his breath. The horse came rolling toward the pair, prostrate on the ground. At the last minute, when it looked like the horse would crush them both, Abe managed to yank Jennie clear.

Jess Hawkins let his breath sigh out with relief. But suddenly, to right and left of the dust cloud raised by the horses' sliding down the slope, puffs of smoke began blossoming, and the reports of rifles reached Jess's ears.

He glanced behind. One man's horse had been creased by a ricochet and was bucking viciously. His rider sailed off on the second jump. One of the others rode after the bucking horse and caught his reins. The sheriff and the others pulled their horses to a halt. Bodine yelled, "Damn it, Hawkins, get out of our line of fire!"

Hawkins knew there was no use going on. He turned his horse at right angles and loped him out of the sheriff's line of fire. He looked back toward Abe and Jennie and the four outlaws.

At this range, accuracy was impossible. Gun muzzles had to be elevated to make the bullets carry the distance. Jess galloped back to the sheriff and his men and yelled, "Damn it, quit shooting! You're as likely to hit the hostages as you are the others!"

The sheriff yelled, "Stop shootin'! It ain't no use!"

Helplessly they sat their horses, staring toward the group at the foot of the slope. The dust cloud raised by their descent was slowly drifting away on the breeze. Suddenly Hawkins saw one of the outlaws leap from his horse. Abe was up, trying to dust himself off. Without warning, the outlaw hit him and knocked him down.

Abe never got a chance to rise. He was yanked to his feet by the outlaw, who looked almost twice his size. Holding Abe with one hand, the big outlaw smashed him rhythmically and systematically until the boy's body slumped and hung helplessly from the outlaw's grasp. Then the big man let him fall. As if still unsatisfied, he kicked Abe viciously in the ribs. He tramped back to his horse and mounted. With his hands he gestured for the others to load Abe on his horse.

Jess Hawkins stood there helplessly, fists clenched so tightly that his forearms ached. He felt light-headed. At that moment there was only one thing he wanted in the world. He wanted a chance at that big outlaw, with fists or guns or clubs or knives or whatever was at hand.

The sheriff said, “Sorry, Hawkins. That was a hell of a thing to have to watch.”

Jess looked at him, surprised. He said, “It would have been worse if they’d known I was along with you and watching it.”

“Sounds like they got reason to be scared of you.”

Jess said, “I wasn’t too damn gentle with the ones I caught.”

One of the men in the posse said, “Are we just goin’ to sit here an’ let ’em get away?”

Bodine said, “What else can we do? They’ll kill them two kids and Donovan if we try to take ’em now.”

“They’re goin’ to kill ’em anyhow. We all know that. I say let’s run ’em down and get it over with. We ain’t never going to get a better chance.”

There was a chorus of agreement from the other men in the posse. The sheriff looked at Hawkins. “They might be right. That bunch is going to kill your boy anyhow. And the girl. And Donovan. It’s just a matter of time.”

Several of the posse said, “Let’s get at it, then. Before they can reach the top of the bluff.”

Hawkins turned his horse. He shifted his rifle slightly until its muzzle pointed loosely toward them. He said harshly, “I’ll kill the first son-of-a bitch that tries.”

Bodine said, “Hawkins, damn it, put that gun down!”

Hawkins said, “Tell ’em, Bodine. I mean what I say.”

“They’ll kill you. You can’t get ’em all.”

“I can get a couple. Do any of you want to try guessing which two it’s going to be?”

For a long time they stared at him, and be stared back. The only sounds were those made by the fidgeting horses and their swishing tails. A fly buzzed around Hawkins’ head.

He wanted to look behind and see how far up the slope the outlaws were. But he didn't move.

He didn't know how long it was. A minute or two maybe. It seemed like ten. Finally one man growled, "Ah, hell, it's too damn late now, anyway."

Hawkins let himself relax. He turned his head. The outlaws were more than halfway up the slope. They could be out on top before the posse could overtake them.

Jennie was riding alone, on the horse previously ridden by her grandfather. Donovan and Abe rode Abe's horse, with Donovan steadying the boy, who still seemed limp.

Several of the posse cursed bitterly. But they were careful to make their curses general, not to direct them straight at Jess. At a plodding walk, the sheriff moved out again, and the others followed him.

Consciousness was slow coming back to Abe. He felt Donovan's strong arm steadying him, and be felt the motion of the horse. Then he remembered. He'd tried to get away with Jennie, but the horse had fallen and thrown them off. Kruse had beaten him before he hardly knew what was going on. His mouth felt numb and swollen; his front teeth ached as if they were loose. There was a sharp pain in his ribs where he had been kicked, and his wounded leg had begun to bleed again. The fall from the horse must have broken loose the scab.

Donovan said, "Comin' out of it, are you? How do you feel?"

Abe turned his head and winced with the pain of doing it. He said, "Awful."

Donovan said, "You tried. For that I thank you. But

for Jennie you'd have made it too."

"I hope you don't think . . . I mean, I figured you'd want me to get Jennie away if I could."

"You done right. Don't worry about that."

Abe glanced at the shadows on the ground. The sun was low in the western sky. They wouldn't camp until dark, and they might not camp then, but sooner or later they would, and that would be the time of greatest danger for Jennie.

He felt more depressed than he had ever felt before. It didn't seem like he could do anything right. If he hadn't interfered with his father, they wouldn't be in the mess right now. His father would not be dead. Jennie and her grandfather would be safe back at their ranch.

He hadn't even been able to ride down that slope successfully. But it was too late now for regrets. What was done was done.

Abe's whole body hurt, bruised as it was from the fall and the beating given him by Kruse. He stared ahead at Jennie. He supposed she was angry at him, because she didn't look at him. She probably was angry because he had ridden off with her, leaving her grandfather at the mercy of the outlaws. But there hadn't been any choice, and Abe knew, if she did not, that Donovan would have been safer if he had been the only hostage than he was this way, being only one of three. He wished he could explain that to her, but it would probably be a long time before he got the chance.

The sun sank down behind the horizon, staining the clouds briefly before they faded to gray. The sky grew darker, until the shapes of horses and riders were only blurs. The stars came out, but still Kruse rode on. Abe figured that he wanted to increase his lead on the sheriff's posse by several miles. He knew the posse wouldn't follow after they were unable to see the trail.

They rode for about ten miles before they stopped. When they did, Kruse said harshly, "No fires. Get yourselves some cold grub and turn in. Well be ridin' before daylight tomorrow. Gore, you keep watch until midnight, and then wake Helfer up."

There was a brief flurry of activity as horses were unsaddled, led away, and staked out. Without fires, it was difficult to tell one man from another. Donovan and Jennie found each other, though, and Donovan helped Jennie to make her bed. He lay down nearby.

Abe felt alone. He wished he could talk to Jennie and explain what he had done, but he knew it was impossible. He staked out his horse, got his blanket roll from behind the saddle, and stretched out. He could see the figure of Gore against the sky, standing with his rifle between the camp and the sheriff's posse behind.

Abe went to sleep. The ground was hard, and he ached, but the long day, the fall from the horse, and the subsequent beating had taken their toll. He slept. Awakened by Jennie's muffled sobs sometime later, he came instantly to his feet, throwing his blanket back.

Even in the darkness he could see the figures of Jennie and a man struggling on the ground. He could hear the sounds of exertion from the man, and muffled sounds from Jennie, over whose mouth the man's hand was clamped. He could hear the tearing sounds as the clothes were ripped from her.

Abe didn't stop to think how foolish interference was. He rushed toward the struggling pair.

Donovan beat him there. With a rock fisted in his hand, he hit the outlaw on the side of the head. The man fell away from Jennie, momentarily stunned, and she began scrambling along the ground, trying to get away.

She was panting with exertion and terror, but she was sobbing too, like a hurt animal.

So quickly did it happen that Abe was still a dozen feet away when flame lanced out wickedly from the muzzle of the outlaw's gun. Ahead of him, Donovan pitched forward, lost immediately to Abe's sight when he fell to the ground and his body blended with the blackness there.

Behind Abe a voice roared, "Gore, goddamn you, put that gun away!"

The voice came from Kruse, awakened by the shot. He knew, apparently, what had happened, because he knew Gore. Abe didn't try attacking Gore. Doing so would help nobody, not Jennie, not Donovan. Instead he knelt beside Donovan and asked, "Mr. Donovan? Where are you hit?"

He got no reply. Jennie, with her clothes half ripped off, now came scrambling to Donovan's side. "Grandpa! Grandpa! Are you all right?" Hysterical, she flung herself down beside him, laying her fearful face against his whiskered one.

Abe pushed himself away to get out of her way. He couldn't be sure, but he thought Donovan was dead.

There was a sudden fury in him that must have been like the fury his father had felt when he found Abe's mother and sisters dead. And for the first time, Abe understood his father's burning thirst for vengeance that could be satisfied by only the most grisly of atrocities committed against the murderers.

Kruse came and stood over Donovan. He knelt and put a hand on Donovan's throat, ignoring the sobbing girl. When he rose, he said, "He's dead."

Jennie's sobbing didn't change. She knew, thought Abe. She had known from the moment she had thrown herself down beside Donovan.

Kruse suddenly rushed at Gore. The sound of his fist striking was like the sound of a cleaver striking a meat cutting block. Gore went back and down as if he had been hit by a club. He wasn't out, though, and he came up to his hands and knees. Kruse said furiously, "Point that goddamn gun at me, and I'll gut-shoot you!"

There was a moment's silence. Then Kruse turned toward the other men, sitting up in their beds. He said with hard menace, "The next son-of-a-bitch that tries to mess with that girl is dead! Why the hell do you think I brought hostages along? There's ten men in back of us, and we're only four. The hostages are the only reason we're still alive. Now, by God, Gore, you get somethin' to dig with and put Donovan underground. And hide the grave so's they won't find him when they pass by here tomorrow."

He stooped down and yanked Jennie away from the body of her grandfather. He said brutally, "He's dead. There ain't no use in you carryin' on forever over him. Get away, so's Gore can bury him."

She fought him, and he cuffed her on the side of the head. She fell. Abe, fists clenched, started toward Kruse. He stopped himself before he reached the man. Tackling Kruse would only get him another beating like the one he'd had yesterday. And it wouldn't help.

So instead he went to Jennie and pulled her away from the body of her grandfather. Numbly she began trying to repair the damage to her clothes.

Abe got her far enough away so that she couldn't hear their talk or the sounds they made. Then he turned his back to her and let her do what she could to fix the way she looked.

He hadn't understood the depths of his father's hatred

of these men before, but now he did. And he wished desperately that he had the last few weeks to live over again.

CHAPTER 17

JESS HAWKINS KNEW EXACTLY WHAT THE OUTLAWS would do as soon as darkness fell. They'd keep going, knowing the posse had to stop. They'd put five, maybe ten miles between them, and it would take hard traveling tomorrow for the posse to catch up.

Bodine also knew, but as soon as he could no longer see the trail, he stopped. "No use goin' on. If they turn and we lose the trail, we'll lose a lot more time tomorrow tryin' to find it again."

Nobody argued much. They were tired, most of them being townsmen and not used to spending whole days in the saddle. Their rumps and thighs were saddle sore. Most of them were already riding partially turned in the saddle, occasionally changing sides, to spare their saddle sores.

Stiffly they dismounted and stiffly took care of their horses, unsaddling and picketing them a sufficient distance from camp to assure a plentiful supply of grass. Each man had his own rations, and there was no reason why they couldn't have fires. In a few minutes there were three of them.

Hawkins still had some deer meat in his saddlebags, though it was getting pretty ripe. He tried to ignore the smell, cut off some thick slices, and spitted them to cook over one of the fires. The two other men using the fire wrinkled their noses at the smell and moved upwind. One said, "How the hell can you eat that stuff?"

Hawkins said, "I'm hungry."

They didn't offer to share with him. They kept watching him warily, and he wondered what was on their minds.

He didn't have long to wait. One asked finally, "What about them rewards? You figure you're entitled to part of them?"

Jess said, "I don't want none of them."

"You willing to sign a paper that says you don't?"

Jess said coldly, "My word is good enough."

"'Course it is. We ain't questioning that." The man didn't bring up the subject of the paper again.

Jess thought sourly that money was all they were interested in. That applied to the sheriff too. None of them cared what the men had done or what they were likely to do farther south if they weren't caught. If it wasn't for the rewards, they'd all be sitting on their butts back in town right now.

He'd been right in not going to the sheriff back home. But he'd been wrong in trying to make each outlaw he caught suffer as much as possible before he died. Doing that had been responsible for the conflict between Abe and himself. It was responsible for Abe's wound, for his being a hostage, for the fact that Donovan and Jennie were also hostages. If he'd been satisfied to kill each man he caught cleanly and quickly, they might now all be dead, Abe safe, and this nightmare of pursuit over and done.

He finished eating. He had been using his blanket in place of a saddle between the horse's back and his rump, mostly for lack of a better way to carry it. Now he carried it well away from camp, spread it on the ground, and lay down. With hands clasped behind his head, he stared moodily toward the three fires and the men moving back and forth within the camp.

He was terrified for Abe. He knew the outlaws wouldn't hesitate to kill him when they no longer had use for him. His mind was like a squirrel in a cage, going back and forth and back and forth, trying to find some way out of this. But there was no way. Eventually the posse would tire of trailing the outlaws, and then they'd move in, disregarding the hostages. When that happened, Abe, Jennie, and Donovan would die. Along with the outlaws. Along with some of the posse.

As soon as the sheriff and his men seemed to be asleep, Jess got up. He left his blanket where it was. Walking silently in the high grass, he went to where he had picketed his horse. The animal was out away from the others, so he didn't disturb them when he pulled the picket pin and swung to the bare back of the Indian pony. The animal had not liked his smell at first but was now used to him.

Hawkins walked him until he was far enough away from camp so that he would not be heard. Then he lined out straight south at a lope, using the stars as his guide. Maybe the outlaws had changed course, but he doubted it. He might not find them, but it was worth a try.

At this steady gait he traveled for six or seven miles. Then he slowed. They'd camp in a low place, probably near water, he reasoned, or someplace where they could at least dig for it in a dry stream bed. So he stayed on the ridges, straining his eyes ahead for the winking spark of a fire in the distance ahead of him.

He saw nothing. He traveled two or three more miles. Then, suddenly, he heard a gunshot on his right. He halted, listening.

He heard no more gunshots. But faintly, carried to him on the breeze, he heard shouting. He had found them, he realized. But who had been shot? Could it have been Abe?

The thought made a cold ball of ice form in his belly. He turned his horse and headed in the direction of the sounds. There was a lot more shouting. He tied his horse to a stout clump of brush and approached the camp on foot.

The outlaws' horses were picketed fairly close to their camp. Jess was able to get close enough to hear Jennie sobbing, and to hear a murmur of talk.

The temptation was great to slip into the camp and kill as many of them as he could before they got him. But he resisted it. There were four of them. He might get two, but the other two would get both him and Abe while he was doing it. So he waited, hesitating, wishing he could do something but knowing there was nothing he could do right now. They'd have a man on guard. That was a certainty.

Grumbling, the outlaws settled down to sleep. Except for one. He got up ponderously from where he had been squatting. There was a burden on his back, recognizable even in darkness and from a distance of over a hundred yards as a body.

In the faint light from the stars, the man came straight toward Jess, who was on the far side of a little dry creek bed. Jess waited, hidden by shadows, his rifle cocked and in his hands. The man came on, as if he had seen Jess.

But Jess knew that he had not. He couldn't. Besides that, if he had, he'd have dropped his burden and gone for his gun.

Not ten yards from Jess the man suddenly bent and let the body fall to the ground. In that instant Jess knew it wasn't Abe. It was Donovan.

He wasn't proud of the relief that surged through him like a flood. But he couldn't help it. The big man was evidently going to try covering the body, because he began trying to break a heavy branch from a scrubby tree.

This was the only chance he was going to get, thought Jess. This chance to get one man and cut the number of the outlaws down to three. Like a cat, he approached the outlaw. He wanted to shove his gun muzzle right against him so that it would deaden the sound of the shot. Otherwise, he'd likely get no chance to get away.

He was three feet away when the man heard him and whirled. Jess didn't hesitate. He shoved the gun muzzle against the man and fired.

He'd intended to put his bullet through the man's chest, but as the man turned he also straightened from a partly crouched position. He took the bullet in his belly, and grunted heavily before he began to fall.

The shot had been only a muffled one. Jess turned immediately and ran, not worrying now about the noise. If he was heard, those in camp would suppose it was the outlaw still trying to break off a branch.

But from a hundred feet away, he turned his head. Against the white of the sand in the bottom of the dry stream bed, he could see the outlaw staggering toward camp. He was bent over, probably hugging his belly with his arms. He made no sound. At least not right away. But suddenly, as he began to climb out of the stream bed, he let loose a roar like that of a wounded bull.

Jess ran as fast as he could toward where he had left his horse. He'd meant to kill the man cleanly and quickly, and had tried to do so, but he couldn't help feeling a certain satisfaction at the knowledge that he had gut-shot him instead. The man would die, but slowly and in pain. He would last out the night, hurting each minute of it. In the morning he would probably be dead.

Furthermore, Jess doubted if Kruse would retaliate against the two hostages that remained. With only two of his men left, he needed hostages more than he ever had.

Gore's shout awakened Kruse, who had immediately gone back to sleep. He was on his feet instantly, gun in hand. Gore came stumbling into camp and collapsed. Kruse cursed and went to where he lay. "What the hell's the matter with you?"

Gore's voice was tight with pain. "Gut-shot. That son-of-a-bitch is still on our trail."

"He's dead. We ain't seen him for days."

Gore's only answer was a groan. Helfer was up now, and so was García. Kruse said, "It ain't possible. We ain't seen him for days."

Abe, also awakened by Gore's shout, felt a wild surge of hope in spite of his grogginess. Maybe his father was, as Gore said, alive.

Gore groaned, "Water. Get me some water."

García said, "That's the worst thing you can give him, if he's gut-shot."

Kruse said, "Give him a canteen."

Abe understood immediately. Kruse knew Gore wasn't going to make it unless he was taken to a town where a doctor or somebody could take care of him, and he had no intention of taking him anywhere. Kruse would leave him to die as he had another of his men farther north. If he wasn't already dead by the time morning came.

At least, thought Abe, Gore wasn't going to bother Jennie anymore. He knew he ought to be ashamed of that thought, but he wasn't. He wasn't even ashamed of being glad Gore was in such pain. He caught himself hoping that Gore didn't die too soon.

Lying there thinking about it, he realized that he hadn't heard a shot. Instead, he'd been awakened by Gore's shout. There was only one explanation why he hadn't heard the shot. The gun had been jammed tight against Gore when it was fired, effectively muffling the sound.

Then his father *must* be alive. The sheriff wouldn't have been out there alone waiting for one of the outlaws to wander away from camp. Neither would any of the sheriff's posse.

His relief was so great that it made him weak. He could feel tears burning his eyes, and he stared up at the sky and thanked the Lord for sparing his father's life.

Gore was cursing now, bitterly, using words Abe had never even heard. Kruse told him sourly to shut up, that he wanted to sleep. Gore cursed him even more bitterly than be had been cursing the man who had put the bullet into him.

Kruse got up. He walked to where Gore was. "You son-of-a-bitch, shut up or I'll shut you up."

Gore quieted. Kruse went back to bed. García and Helfer were utterly silent, probably thinking that, had it been one of them instead of Gore who had been shot, they would now be getting the same callous treatment from Kruse. But neither of them protested. Neither got up to go to Gore and see if he wanted anything; they knew he was dying and would not last the night.

The camp quieted, except for the slight sounds of Helfer pacing back and forth. Jennie's bed was about ten feet away from Abe's. He could hear her muffled sobs. She was not only terrified, he thought, but she was grieving for her grandfather. He wished he could go to her and comfort her, but he knew anything he did would probably be misunderstood. Besides, there was no use bringing the wrath of Kruse down on them.

So he lay still, staring at the stars. It was a long time before Jennie quieted. He could hear Kruse snoring, and once in a while García grunted and turned over. Helfer wasn't pacing anymore, but Abe could see his silhouette against the stars, rifle in his hands.

Finally he slept, and it seemed only an instant before Kruse's harsh voice woke him up.

The sky was turning gray. He got up, rolled his blanket, and tied it behind his saddle, along with that of Jennie. No fires were built. Nobody ate or mentioned it. Horses were brought in, saddled, and made ready. Kruse said, "All right, let's get out of here."

Jennie's voice shook as she said, "My grandpa. Aren't you even going to bury him?"

Kruse said, "What for? The sheriff will do it."

Abe whispered in her ear. "Let it go. He's right. The sheriff will do it a lot better than these outlaws will."

She quieted. Kruse led out. Again, Abe and Jennie followed him. The other two brought up the rear, one trailing the horse Donovan had ridden yesterday, with Gore's dead body slung across the saddle.

CHAPTER 18

JESS HAWKINS RETURNED TO CAMP WITHOUT BEING either seen or heard. He pulled off his boots, lay down, and pulled the blanket over him. He'd be tired today, because it was already nearly dawn, but it would be worth it. He'd eliminated another of the killers.

He could only guess why Donovan had been killed. Most likely one of the outlaws had attacked Jennie, or tried to, and Donovan had intervened. He hoped that Abe had joined him in trying to protect Jennie, and for several moments he had mixed feelings about that. If Abe had first come to Jennie's aid, he would be dead instead of Donovan. But perhaps, he thought, both had tried to help her, and only Donovan had been killed.

In any case, he had avenged Donovan by killing the man assigned to bury him, probably the same one who had killed him. It would be logical for the outlaw leader to force Donovan's killer to bury him.

He finally slept, and it seemed only an instant before dawn woke him up. The others were already stirring around the camp. Hawkins decided to keep what had happened last night to himself, for now, at least. They'd all find out soon enough. They'd find Donovan's body and the outlaw who had been shot.

They did without breakfast and rode out as soon as it was light enough to trail. Bodine set the pace, a fast one but consistent with maintaining the horses' strength. It was trot, and walk, and lope, and walk. Every hour they stopped for five minutes, loosened the cinches, and let the horses rest. Hawkins had to admire the way Bodine handled it, and his respect for the sheriff went up a notch. Bodine knew they'd lost a lot of ground last night. He wanted to make it up if he didn't have to exhaust the horses doing it.

The sun was hardly more than up when they reached the camp the outlaws had made last night. The outlaw Hawkins had shot was gone. Pretending to scout around, Hawkins found Donovan's body and called the sheriff to where it was. Bodine said, "What do you reckon happened here last night?"

Hawkins shrugged. "Maybe Donovan tried to protect his granddaughter. Looks like he got killed for his pains."

Bodine nodded, apparently not wondering why Donovan's body was found so far from camp. He probably assumed Donovan had been dragged there just to get him out of camp.

Bodine assigned a man to bury Donovan, telling him that when he had finished he could either try catching up or go back to town. The man said he thought he'd go back if Bodine would still give him his share of the reward. He seemed relieved to be able to.

They went on right away, maintaining the same succession of gaits, and near noon they spotted the outlaws and their hostages ahead. Slowly they gained, but when they were a mile behind, Bodine slowed the pace. Unexpectedly, the outlaws also began to lag, and finally, coming to the edge of a deep ravine cut by floods, Hawkins saw them halted on the other side less than three hundred yards away.

Bodine said, "What the hell? Ain't that a body layin' across that horse?"

Hawkins didn't reply, because a shout came echoing across the ravine. "Hey! We know you got Hawkins there with you! Give him up, and you can have Gore's body to take back for the reward!"

Bodine waited a moment. Then he shouted, "And if we don't?"

"We'll keep the son-of-a-bitch with us until he rots. Or we'll bury him so's you'll never find the grave."

Hawkins shifted his rifle slightly and let his horse dance away from the posse. He didn't think the sheriff would go for a deal like that, but he wasn't so sure of the men he had along with him.

Bodine yelled back, "Give us some time to talk about it."

"Two minutes! That's all you got!"

Bodine spoke without turning his head. "Get ready to jump off your horses and open up on them. I don't want any wild shooting, but if we can get one more of them, we'd be that much ahead."

Hawkins said angrily, "The distance is three hundred yards, and Donovan's girl and my boy ain't ten feet away from them!"

Bodine, ignoring him, said, "Now!" Instantly the members of the posse leaped from their horses. Bodine yelled, "Smathers, Rodrigues, get them damn horses out of here before one of 'em gets hit."

Hawkins swung from his horse. He let the animal go, and the horse followed Smathers and Rodrigues and the horses they were heading back out of range. Gunfire crackled all around him, and answering gunfire began crackling across the ravine. Abe and Jennie were now out of sight, as were the outlaws. The only thing visible across the ravine were occasional puffs of smoke. The outlaws' horses had moved back into heavy brush of their own accord, liking neither the noise of gunfire nor its acrid smell.

Hawkins didn't shoot. He hoped Abe and Jennie had sense enough to keep their heads down. He half-expected to see the two leap up and try escaping again. When they didn't, he decided one of the outlaws must be too close.

At last, after about ten minutes, the outlaw leader's bellow came across the ravine. "Sheriff?"

"What?"

"Quit shootin' and let us get out of here, or, by God, we'll kill one of the hostages!"

Bodine hesitated a moment. Behind him Jones said, "He won't do it. He's just runnin' a bluff. I say let's two or three of us keep 'em pinned down while the others circle around and get 'em from behind."

Bodine said, "That might not be a bad idea. How long do you think it'll take you to get over there?"

"Give us twenty minutes."

Hawkins crawled close to the sheriff and jammed his rifle muzzle into Bodine's side. "Tell him to forget it, Bodine, or, by God, I'll blow a hole in you."

"You wouldn't."

"Wouldn't I? The hostage they're going to kill first is my son. If you think I won't kill you to save my son, then you'd better think again."

Bodine considered that for a minute. Hawkins jabbed the gun muzzle so hard against him that the sheriff winced. He said, "Tell 'em, damn it! Now!"

Bodine looked straight into his eyes. What he saw there apparently changed his mind. He yelled, "Hold your fire! Let 'em go!"

The fire slackened, but only momentarily. Hawkins grated, "You'd better sound more convincing, sheriff. Like your life depended on them doing what you say."

The sheriff yelled again. This time there was a frantic urgency in his voice that was unmistakable. The firing stopped.

Across the ravine, the outlaws lost no time. Herding Jennie and Abe before them, the three scuttled to safety behind the screen of brush that rimmed the ravine.

Jess Hawkins got slowly to his feet. He lowered his gun.

He was unprepared for the fury Bodine turned on

him. Bodine's fist struck him squarely in the mouth and sent him staggering back. Before he could recover, Bodine was on him like an animal. He knocked Hawkins back bodily, and both crashed to the ground.

Hawkins understood that this was no fight to the death where guns would be used. Bodine was simply taking out on him the frustration that had built up in him during the chase. They'd had the outlaws pinned down and had had a chance to surround and capture them, thus ending the chase once and for all. Hawkins had prevented it.

But Hawkins welcomed the fight, because it also gave him a chance to work off his own frustrations and nagging fears. He slammed a knee into the sheriffs belly, brought a hoarse grunt from him, then rolled and made it to hands and knees.

Bodine came clawing after him, face contorted, eyes glittering. Hawkins got up, and as Bodine rose, looped a long haymaker that caught the sheriff squarely on the nose. It burst like a tomato, spraying blood all over his face and making tears come gushing to his eyes. But it didn't slow him down. He put down his head and charged like a buffalo, bearing Hawkins back with the sheer force of his rush.

Neither man had noticed, but Hawkins' back was now to the lip of the ravine. Bodine's rush carried him over it, and unable to stop, the sheriff lunged over after him.

There was a sheer drop of ten feet or so, then a steep slope covered with thorny brush. Hawkins hit the slope on his back with enough force to knock the wind out of him completely. He rolled, hit the brush, and was slowed by it, so that he stopped rolling before he had gone a dozen feet.

He heard Bodine grunt explosively as the sheriff hit

the slope immediately behind. The sheriff also rolled, and stopped ten feet or so away.

Both men lay there gasping, trying to refill their lungs. Hawkins' chest was one huge area of pain. He choked and gasped, and thought he was going to die before he got a breath of air. But he didn't die, and eventually he got a little air into his lungs; after that, a little more. He didn't dare wait until he was breathing normally, because the sheriff was coming. He could hear the crashing of the brush.

He met the sheriff head-on, both men clawing through the tangle of thorny brush. Hawkins swung, connected, followed the sheriff as he fell back and again tumbled down the slope. Bodine rolled into a little clearing, regained his feet, and met Hawkins as he came stumbling down the slope with a kick that caught him squarely in the groin.

The sudden stabbing pain left him bent over gasping and weak. The sheriff followed up his advantage and swung a long, looping fist that caught Hawkins in the throat.

That was the end of the fight. Helpless, gasping, choking, Hawkins collapsed to the ground, and lay with knees pulled up against his chest instinctively to protect himself.

Bodine aimed a kick at him, but stopped it before it landed. He said disgustedly, "Ah, hell! What's the use?" For several moments he stood there, dragging noisy, harsh breaths of air into his lungs. Then he bent and took Hawkins' arm. "Come on. I guess I ain't mad no more."

Hawkins let Bodine help him to his feet. He was glad enough to call it quits. He doubted if he'd ever breathe normally again. He doubted if that awful pain in his belly would ever go away.

Side-by-side the two clawed their way through the heavy brush and up the slope. At the foot of the drop they turned and traveled parallel to the edge of the ravine for about a hundred feet before they found a place that would permit them to climb out.

On top again, the two mounted their horses, which members of the posse brought to them. Hawkins knew he was grimy and that his clothes had been torn in half a dozen places by the brush. He was bloody from Bodine's nose and from a blow Bodine had landed on his mouth.

But strangely enough, he felt better. The tension of the long, bitter chase had momentarily been released.

CHAPTER 19

SHERIFF BODINE LED THE CAVALCADE DOWN INTO THE brush-choked ravine and out on the other side. Reaching the level plain, they could see the outlaws about a mile ahead.

Hawkins, riding half a dozen yards behind Bodine, could feel the hostile stares of the posse. He understood how bitterly they resented being stopped from finishing the chase back there once and for all. They were tired and saddle-sore, and they were a long way from home. They knew they could kill or capture the outlaws anytime they chose. All that was holding them back was danger to the hostages held by the three remaining escapees.

He admitted to himself that he wasn't going to be able to hold them back again. Tonight they'd balk at spending another day on the trail. They'd insist on attacking the outlaw camp, whatever the consequences for Jennie Donovan and Abe. And the trouble was, Hawkins couldn't blame them very much. In their place, he'd probably have felt the same. They knew as well as he did that if the outlaws got away they'd kill the hostages anyway.

The day dragged on. Nobody talked, each of the men still nursing a smoldering anger. In midafternoon Hawkins pulled up beside Bodine and said, "They ain't going to hold back again."

"I know it."

"How about you and me going in ahead of them? If that bunch charges into the outlaw camp, they'll likely kill everything that moves. Especially if it's dark."

Bodine thought about that for a minute or two. Finally he nodded. "All right. But I ain't going to lie to them. I'll tell them you and me are going in first, but that they're to come on when they hear gunfire."

Hawkins nodded with relief. "Fair enough."

Bodine's nose was swelled double its normal size. One of his eyes was black and swelled nearly shut. Hawkins said, "You sure look like hell."

The sheriff grinned. "You ought to see yourself."

For a while they rode in silence. Finally the sheriff said, "Maybe we can surprise 'em. Maybe we can still save your boy and Donovan's girl."

Hawkins nodded. He didn't really think they could, but he had to admit that there had never been too much chance of saving either one. When the outlaw camp was attacked, when they saw the hostages weren't providing protection to them, they'd kill them out of pure viciousness. They didn't have anything to lose. They'd killed Donovan and thus were all guilty of a murder that could be proved. The penalty for three murders was the same as for one.

But now, after all this time, Hawkins reached a decision. Not again would he try to make the outlaws' dying slow and as painful as he could. This time he would shoot to kill instantly if possible. He was interested now only in saving the lives of Abe and Jennie Donovan.

The day waned, and the sun sank in the western sky. It set, and dyed the clouds, and the world gradually turned gray that deepened into dusk.

While it still was barely light, Bodine halted. "Get yourselves something quick to eat. We're goin' on tonight. Hawkins and me are going on ahead to scout their camp. If you hear shootin', come a-runnin'. Understand?"

The posse agreed, their relief obvious. Hawkins didn't have time to cook any of his nearly rotten meat, so he accepted some dried biscuits and raw bacon from the sheriff's hoard. He choked it down, drinking water to make the task easier. He was ready before the others were.

Bodine finally mounted up. He looked at the posse. "Get yourselves a bearing on a star. Come on at a walk. Likely them outlaws will go five or ten miles before they stop, but no noise and no talking. Like I said, come a-runnin' when you hear guns going off."

Hawkins led out, holding his Indian pony to a trot. Bodine kept pace a few yards behind. Hawkins picked himself a star over in the west, a bright one, marking where it was in relation to his heading.

Neither man talked. Hawkins discovered that he was glad it was almost over now. He was glad, even if he got killed. And he doubted if Abe would be in any more danger when they attacked the outlaws' camp than he had been in all along. Last night one of the outlaws had tried molesting Jennie, and Donovan had died defending her. Tonight it might happen again, only tonight if anyone was killed defending Jennie, it would be Abe.

They maintained a steady trot. After they bad gone what Hawkins judged was five miles, he let his horse slow to a walk. Now, every few hundred yards he stopped and listened carefully before going on. There were two reasons for doing so. He didn't want to blunder into the outlaws' camp unexpectedly. Nor did he want to be surprised by Bodine's posse catching up from behind.

Finally, when he judged they were nearly ten miles from where they'd left the others, he heard a voice from almost straight ahead.

He swung down from his horse immediately, and the sheriff followed suit. They found brush clumps stout enough to hold the horses, and tied them. Without speaking, they went on afoot.

Hawkins realized that he had come full circle since he'd discovered his wife and twin daughters killed. From handling it himself, from dealing out his own savage retribution, he was now willing to entrust it to the law. Further, he didn't thirst any more for the agony of the dying outlaws, agony that would match that suffered by his wife. He discovered that he only wanted this to be over with. He wanted to go home. He wanted to live for something besides the deaths of other human beings. And he wanted Abe and Jennie both to come with him. Someone would have to take care of Jennie, and it might as well be him and Abe. Maybe Abe and Jennie would want to get married later on.

He heard another voice ahead, much closer now. Off to his right, he heard the sound of a horse moving about. He put a hand on the sheriff's arm. He gestured to the right, and the sheriff moved away. Hawkins himself angled slightly left.

He was walking now as slowly and as silently as any Indian ever had. Each footstep was tested before his weight went down, to be sure no branch would crack. His eyes were narrowed, trying to pierce the darkness ahead of him. Even his nostrils were flared, testing the breeze for smells.

It was dark, too dark for accurate shooting, but he knew that if he and Bodine failed to kill the three outlaws immediately, it would be too late for Jennie and for Abe.

A careful step at a time, he reached the edge of their camp. They had no fire. They were only shadows out there in the darkness. Fortunately, they were in a little clearing where there was enough starlight for him to distinguish faint shapes.

Hawkins stood frozen there less than fifty feet away. He hoped the sheriff would stay put, at least for a minute or two. If they both stood still and listened carefully, they might be able to spot the outlaws and distinguish them from the hostages.

Hawkins heard a rambled growl, "Now, let that damned girl alone!" It came from a blurred shape that nearly blended with the ground. Hawkins guessed the outlaw leader was settling down to sleep.

He knew he didn't dare wait any longer. The sheriff might start blazing away at any moment, and when he did, the posse would come galloping. God only knew how far away they were right now. They might be as close as a couple of hundred yards.

He could get the big outlaw, and after that he'd just have to do the best he could. He launched himself like a springing mountain lion, rifle held before him in both hands. He closed with the blurred shape on the ground, and the man came up with the sharp exclamation, "What the hell? Who . . .?"

He never finished the question. Hawkins swung the rifle savagely, and its butt came solidly against the big outlaw's head. There was a feel to the impact, a kind of give that told Hawkins he had crushed the outlaw's skull.

Off-balance as the outlaw fell away from him, he staggered forward, trying to keep his feet. He bawled, "Abe? Where you at?"

The sheriff might have been ready to open fire, but that shout stopped whatever action he might have taken. Hawkins heard his son's answering, startled shout, placed it, and charged instantly against a moving shape headed toward the sound. A gun flared, and something like a hot iron burned along Hawkins' ribs. He knew he was hit, and didn't know yet how bad, but his rush couldn't now be stopped. He closed with the outlaw as the gun flashed again, swinging the rifle by its barrel like a club. He heard the sound of its striking just after he felt another bullet catch his shoulder with an impact like the kick of a mule. Again something snapped under the rifle's force, and Hawkins thought this time it must have been the outlaw's neck.

Still moving, avoiding the falling body of the outlaw, he roared, "Abe! Where the hell's the other one?"

Abe couldn't answer, but Jennie did. Her scream was blood-curdling in the darkness, a lost scream of terror, and Jess Hawkins immediately swung that way. He heard Bodine yell, "Hawkins? Where the hell are you? I can't see good enough to shoot!"

He ignored the sheriff's question. He had no time to answer it. He was afraid that Abe would be dead when he reached him, but he kept going anyway, praying silently to himself.

Jennie screamed again. Then Jess Hawkins charged into a tangle of struggling bodies, fell over them, and groped for the outlaw, immediately distinguishable because of his small size and also because of the Spanish curse that came from his mouth.

The outlaw knew there was no use surrendering. He turned on Jess, whose shoulder was turning numb, whose whole side was soaked with blood. He turned, and a knife blade flashed in the starlight, and Hawkins felt it bite deep into his thigh. Then he had the man's wrist in both his hands.

Somewhere the sheriff roared, "Hawkins? Where the hell are you?"

Hawkins couldn't answer immediately, but his son could and did. He yelled, "Over here!" Abe was circling the struggling pair, his father's rifle in both his hands, trying for a chance either to hit the outlaw with it or to shoot. Hawkins, still struggling for the knife, heard the sheriff say, "Which is which, for Christ's sake?"

Hawkins found his voice. "Make up your goddamn mind and do it fast! I'm shot and cut, and I'm barely keepin' this son-of-a-bitch from cuttin' me again!"

His voice told both Abe and the sheriff which was which. He heard the sound of rifle butt meeting flesh and bone, and the outlaw's arm suddenly went limp. Jess Hawkins struggled to his feet.

He heard the thunder of approaching hooves, and suddenly the little clearing was filled with lunging horses, their riders shouting questions, until the sheriff roared at them to shut up and build a fire so that he could see.

Jess felt weak. His whole leg was soaked with blood

from the knife wound. His side was warm and wet from the bullet burn along his ribs. His shoulder had no feeling in it at all. But it would. It would, soon enough.

He sat down heavily. Abe asked worriedly, “Pa, how bad you hurt?”

Hawkins grunted, “Not so bad but what I’ll heal.” He sounded cross, and he sounded sour, but inside him it was like the sun rising in the morning after a night of rain.

His son was alive, and Jennie was safe. He himself was alive. The job of vengeance was done, and now they would all be going home.

We hope that you enjoyed reading this
Sagebrush Large Print Western.
If you would like to read more Sagebrush titles,
ask your librarian or contact the Publishers:

United States and Canada

Thomas T. Beeler, *Publisher*
Post Office Box 659
Hampton Falls, New Hampshire 03844-0659
(800) 818-7574

United Kingdom, Eire, and
the Republic of South Africa

Isis Publishing Ltd
7 Centremead
Osney Mead
Oxford OX2 0ES England
(01865) 250333

Australia and New Zealand

Bolinda Publishing Pty. Ltd.
17 Mohr Street
Tullamarine, 3043, Victoria, Australia
(016103) 9338 0666